THE RULES OF THE GAME

"My insurance provides triple indemnity for whoever does the actual treework. The clause becomes effective the moment he begins a tree, remains in effect till he finishes it, and stipulates that he remain in the tree throughout that time. Ordinarily that doesn't pose much of a problem. Only very rarely have we encountered jobs that required more than a day. The biggest tree we ever felled only took two. We figure four days for this one, but even so, Tom will only have to spend three nights in it, and he'll have a tree tent to sleep in and a portable campfire to keep him warm." She winked at Strong. "And if the Good Fates please, a dryad to keep him company . . ."

The Last Yggdrasill

Robert F. Young

A Del Rey Book

BALLANTINE BOOKS • NEW YORK

A Del Rey Book
Published by Ballantine Books

Library of Congress Catalog Card Number: 81-22840

ISBN 0-345-30420-9

Manufactured in the United States of America

First Edition: May 1982

Cover art by Michael Herring

In Scandinavian mythology the great evergreen ash, Yggdrasill, was the tree of life and knowledge, the tree of grief and fate, the tree of time and space—the tree of the universe. It had three roots. One of them extended down into Niflheim and one stretched to Jotunheim. The third emerged in Asgard, near the fountain of Urd, where the gods sat in judgment and to which they rode daily over the Bifrost Bridge of the rainbow.

Prologue

Come, my sisters, let us bring our journey to an end and settle here. The land is vast and the soil is rich and the terrain is ideal. And there are dwellers.

But, Xtil, are the dwellers amenable to our needs?

Yes. They are a simple folk. See the mud huts in which they live?

But, Xtil, they will not remain simple.

No, but they will remain so for a long time. We must take advantage of that time. We are the last of our kind, and it will avail us nothing to look farther. . . . Come, let us become our other selves. Let us know the rush of the wind and the warmth of the sun and the sweetness of the rain.

Xtil, we are afraid.

Do not be. All beings must someday die. Come, let us live while we can as we were meant to live!

Yes, Xtil—yes!

Spread out then, my sisters, and be free!

I

Yggdrasill astralis
Habitat: NW New America, Plains (Genji 5)
Population: 1

YOU were always aware of the tree's presence, even when you turned your back on it and walked to the very outskirts of the village that encircled it, even when you walked miles out into the vast fields of wheat that encircled the village like an inland sea. When you stood in the village square, as Strong stood now, it overwhelmed you. Its foliage was a great, green cloud, its trunk a bleak, black cliff.

Ever since the tree crew's arrival, Strong had been unable to get the tree out of his mind. Everywhere he went, the tree went with him. He knew he was afraid, but he knew also that his fear did not wholly account for the tree's omnipresence, for he was always afraid before a felling. There was another factor involved. It was as though the tree were indivisible from the village, from the vast grain-covered plain, from the planet itself. Certainly it was indivisible from his future.

Properly speaking, the village square was a circle, but the colonists who had expropriated the enchanting houses surrounding it and who comprised the Triumvirate-subsidized Co-operative did not think of it as such. Strong did not think of it as such either. Villages do not have circles at their centers, even when they circle the circles; even when their streets radiate from them like the spokes of a wheel. Villages, traditionally, have squares. Ergo, Strong was standing in the village square.

The colonists had named the village Bigtree, and they had named the territory in the midst of which it stood Kansasia. They had named themselves too. They called themselves The Reapers, a term inspired less by the wheat they harvested than by the money it brought in. They also referred to themselves as The Chosen People. It was true they had not been chosen by God, but they had been chosen by the Triumvirate, which amounted to almost the same thing.

The rays of Genji the sun, absent from the square since early morning, were beginning to bathe it once again. The Reapers had long ago leveled the Quantextil burial mounds and had seeded the entire area with grass that was guaranteed to grow in shade, but you could see where the mounds had been because the grass grew greener there. The Reapers had also removed the big birdfeeder in which the Quantextil had fed the birds in winter and perhaps during the rest of the year too, and which had rotted into ruin, but they had allowed the huge stone birdbath to remain. Probably they did not consider the bath to be an inducement for the haha birds to remain, whereas the feeder, had they replaced it with a new one and put feed in it, would have been.

Strong could hear the birds. A few minutes ago a flock of them had winged in from the plain. The birds lived exclusively in the tree and had managed to survive not only the cold months of winter but the war of sticks and stones and acoustical nightmares the Reapers had been waging against them. Now that the tree was destined to die, the war was over, for the tree was the last tree, and when it died the haha birds were doomed.

Strong looked up, up, up into the branches above him, and it was like looking up at the vaulted dome of a cathedral. He could feel the damp coolness of the tree's transpiration. And he could feel his fear. It was a bleak fear—a cold, foreboding temple in the green atmosphere of his thoughts. And he could feel something else. A thought that was not his own? It did not seem to be a thought, and yet it must be.

It was couched in words: *When I die, you die too.*

He turned his back on the tree and began walking out of the square. The tree walked with him. To his left stood the Bigtree Hotel, where he and the rest of the tree crew were the only guests. But he did not go there; instead he entered one of the radiating streets and began walking toward the outskirts of the village. The street was one of those that lay beneath the projected airhauler route, and the houses lining it had been vacated. They were exquisite houses, as were all the houses in the village. It was as though art and architecture had joined hands to create them. To look at one of them was to want to live in it. The natural finish of the wood that comprised the houses glowed with a subdued golden light. Strong could see into some of the backyards. Gaudy lawn furniture struck a discordant note. The small stone birdbaths the Quantextil had left behind in each yard had been converted into charcoal braziers. The Reapers did not like to be reminded that their houses were not nearly as new as they seemed, that for years, perhaps centuries, they had been occupied by ignorant indigenes who worried about the welfare of the haha birds. The Reapers flatly refused to believe AnthropoCo's conclusion that the Quantextil had *built* the houses. A race that had preceded the Quantextil, a *civilized* race, had done the building, they maintained. Their cathexis with respect to civilization was certainly understandable enough. They had been selected for the colony by the branch of the Triumvirate known as the Multinational Office of Extraterrestrial

Lands—MOEL—for their bright brains as well as their green thumbs. All of them were bachelors in agriculture; many of them had degrees in other fields as well. Westermeyer, for example, had a doctor's degree in political science. Westermeyer was the head of the Co-op.

He was with the two other members of the crew and the foreman when Strong entered the corrugated-steel shed on the village's outskirts that the Co-op had partially emptied of grain machinery to provide room for the airhauler. With Peake and Bluesky and Matthews. Peake and Bluesky had been working on the airhauler all day, reassembling it, oiling and adjusting its mechanical parts, and Matthews had come around to check it out. Westermeyer had come with her. Matthews had inherited the tree-removal company from her husband and ran the show on stage rather than from afar. It was a tiny company that belied the corporate-sounding name her husband had given it: TreeCo. She was a thin, wiry woman in her late sixties who wore her undyed graying hair in a ragged bob. In the field, she dressed the same way her three-man tree crew did—in plaid shirt, denim breeches, and calf-high boots. Westermeyer was short, portly, balding, and somewhere in his fifties. Standing next to him, waiting for Matthews to finish her inspection, Bluesky and Peake had the aspect of two tall sticks of wood.

"How's the tree look, Tom?" Bluesky asked.

"Big," Strong said.

"Hell, we knew that," Peake said. The long visor of his cap added to the pronounced angles of his face but did not rob them of their symmetry. "Is that all you learned after gawking at it all afternoon?"

"You know, Mr. Strong," Westermeyer said, "I admire someone with the guts to do what you're going to do. I wouldn't climb up into that damned tree for all the tea there used to be in China!"

"I happened to draw the long blade of grass is all," Strong said. "We always draw lots before a felling," he explained, "only instead of using matches or straws, we use blades of grass."

"It seems to me that by letting chance decide which of you is going to risk his neck, one of you is bound to do more than his share of the risking."

"Eventually it averages out."

"It still strikes me as being unfair."

"They draw to win, Doctor Westermeyer," Matthews said from the airhauler's rear hatchway where she was inspecting the winch. "The man in the tree gets double time."

"Oh. Well, that does throw a somewhat different light on the matter. I can't begin to tell you," Westermeyer went on, "what a relief it's going to be to all of us here in Bigtree to get rid of that damn tree!"

"You ever hear of the buffalo, Doctor Westermeyer?" Bluesky asked.

"I read about them."

"Once there were fifty million of them. When the white man got done slaughtering them there were only five hundred."

"I'm afraid I don't get the connection."

"Fifty million. Think of that."

"Christ, don't start it with that buffalo shit again!" Peake said.

"I didn't start it—the white man did."

"Knock it off, Bluesky," Matthews said.

Bluesky shrugged. "I only mentioned."

Strong said, "I'm going to use the long spurs."

Matthews nodded. "They're safest." She turned the winch motor on, listened for a moment to its smooth *hmhmhm*, then turned it back off. She stepped down from the hatchway. "We'll start with the small tongs," she said. "They'll do for most of the overstory."

The tongs were piled in one corner of the shed along

with the rest of the equipment. Strong looked at them. They were made of lightweight ultrasteel, and there were three pairs. The largest had teeth as long as those of Tyrannosaurus rex. He ran his eyes over the airhauler. Its size belied the fact that when disassembled it fitted into a twelve-by-twelve shipping crate. With its airfloat flexitanks inflated it would look larger yet. At the moment its flutter-wings were folded back along its sides. Their function was to stabilize the craft during a limb lift. When the tanks were inflated, the craft, with its black-and-yellow paint job, would look like a gigantic honeybee.

"Well," Matthews said, wiping her hands on a soilkil rag, "I guess that finishes the prelims."

"It's dinnertime anyway," Westermeyer said. "I told the hotel chef to prepare you people something extra special. It ought to be almost ready to serve by now."

"Let's go get it then," Matthews said. She strode out of the shed.

The Bigtree Hotel had not always been a hotel. Originally it had merely been a house much larger than any of the others. The consensus of opinion among the Reapers was that it had played the role of palace to a long succession of Quantextil chiefs. Whether it had or had not, it had solved the problem of how to accommodate the groups of tourists that 700 Wonders, Inc., began bringing in almost before the Reapers had had a chance to settle down in their new homes. Overnight it had become the Bigtree Hotel.

Accommodating the tourists had been anything but an altruistic gesture on the Reapers' part. In deeding the Co-op the village and the encompassing territory, MOEL had stipulated that the tree remain accessible to the public at all times and that temporary living quarters be made available to any nonresident wishing to view it. However, the gloomy picture had had its bright side: MOEL had neglected to put a price ceiling on such accommodations, and the Reapers had been able to allay part of their resentment over having their privacy invaded by making the sightseers pay through the nose, via 700 Wonders, for every square inch of living space they occupied during their visits.

There were no sightseers now, of course. Putting the village temporarily off-limits had been an inevitable corollary to MOEL's approval of the Co-op's request to remove the tree. Probably there would never be sightseers again, Matthews reflected as she seated herself at the center table in the hotel dining hall. The village was a tourist attraction in its own right, but the tree was the true magnet, and once it was gone, no one was likely to come all the way to Plains just to view houses, however enchanting they might be.

The hollow feeling had come back, she noted as she rearranged the silverware on the placemat before her. During the day, with so much to occupy her, the hollowness had been absent, but now that the day was done and nothing lay before her except dinner and bed, it had returned.

She tried to fill herself with the room. Like the hotel, its present function was not its original one, but it was admirably suited for the use to which the Co-op had put it. Except for Westermeyer, Bluesky, Peake, Strong, and herself, it was empty, but it was capable of accommodating half a hundred diners. The Reapers had installed a bar and a kitchen respectively in two much smaller rooms that adjoined it, but other than furnishing it with tables and chairs they had done nothing to the dining room proper. There was no sign here of the rot that had set in in some of the houses. The floor blended imperceptibly into the walls and the walls blended imperceptibly into the ceiling, the natural grain and tone of the wood as distinct and as deep as though the hotel had been built yesterday. Soft yet radiant light emanated from wall and ceiling areas that had no demarcations other than those established by the light itself. Doorways were exquisite archways that were pauses in rather than interruptions of the walls. On one wall a large mirror threw back a scene more vivid than the real one; on the opposite wall, a large, rectangular window, its single pane so clear as to seem nonexistent, looked out into the darkening square. The floor had a dark, mahoganylike finish, the walls suggested walnut, while the ceiling brought to mind white oak.

But the room, for all its quiet loveliness, failed to fill Matthews, and the hollowness remained. It had been with her ever since her husband died, but his death had precipitated, not authored, it. It was the hollowness that comes with the realization that one's life is empty, and sooner or later it would have come whether her husband had died or not. Even if they had had children it would have come. Although she had not known it, her life had been empty long before his death. It had been empty ever since the morning she had looked at the watercolor she had done the day before and seen with sudden, terrible clarity that it was the work of an amateur who would always be an amateur, that there was no art in it because there was no art in her, only pretension and self-deceit. She had been able to take the insight in her stride then. She had not realized then that her pursuit had come to constitute a psychological nest egg that would see her safely through her final years. She had not realized until her husband died that she was poverty-stricken, that the only assets she had ever had were her youth and beauty, and that her "art" had been a hastily summoned surrogate to fill the void their departure had left.

A fair-haired waitress with milk-white skin began serving the meal. Westermeyer introduced her as Katerina Vanderzee and observed with understandable bitterness that she was one of a dozen Reapers, all with bachelor's degrees, whom the Co-op had had to sacrifice upon the altar of MOEL-mandated tourism. The meal comprised prime ribs of beef, potatoes au gratin, corn on the cob, a tossed salad, bread, and a dessert of strawberry shortcake topped with whipped cream. All the comestibles, except the bread and the biscuits for the shortcake, consisted of or had been derived from produce and meat airtrucked in from elsewhere on Plains. During their two terrestrial years on the planet, the Reapers had concentrated exclusively on the growing of wheat. Wheat, after all, was why they were where they were. A modest flour mill that processed a minute fraction of each crop supplied their baking needs, but otherwise they were dependent for their food on the other Plains colonies. Their bread was their pride and joy. They made nothing but whole wheat, but it had the flavor of enriched white bread. Its nutritious qualities were such, Westermeyer declared, that the time had come when man *could* live on bread alone.

Matthews was unimpressed. "You can get whole-life bread anywhere," she said.

"Not *natural* whole-life bread."

"You don't supplement the flour?"

Westermeyer shook his head. "We don't add a damn thing! I think," he went on, "that you're identifying *our* wheat with ordinary wheat. The wheat *we* grow is unique to New America. We grow two crops a year, thanks partly to the soil but mostly to Plains' year and a half solar orbit. The field team from BotaniCo found it growing wild when they arrived on Plains. But only in and near Kansasia—it grew nowhere else. Superficially it resembles *Triticum compactum*, the terrestrial species the Triumvirate has had the most success with on other umbilical planets, but *Triticum compactum* it is not. It contains everything necessary to sustain human life. That's why the Triumvirate chose and subsidized people like myself and the other Kansasian colonists to cultivate it and to assess the feasibility of someday growing it in other acreages, both here and on other worlds. One loaf of our bread per day," Westermeyer concluded, "contains everything a man needs to keep going for as long as he cares to go."

"Living on bread alone is nothing new," Strong said. "I remember reading a book by Alessandro Manzoni, *I Promessi Sposi*. It's a historical novel about seventeenth-century Italy. In it the peasants ate almost nothing but bread. You could say they lived on bread alone."

"You're talking about fictitious people," Westermeyer said.

"Sure, but they were based on real people. They had a gruel they made by boiling flour and water. It was called *polenta*. I guess they ate it to break the monotony of the bread." Abruptly Strong realized that everyone was looking at him, even Katerina who stood nearby, and he stopped talking and returned his eyes to his plate.

Matthews noticed his discomfiture. Poor Tom, she thought. Aloud, she said, "What about the Quantextil, Doctor Westermeyer? Did *they* live on bread alone?"

"According to AnthropoCo, they did. I daresay they lived long lives too. Except the last generation."

"Why'd they migrate to the north and kill themselves in the Death Caves?" Peake asked.

"Nobody knows for certain."

"Maybe they ran outta bread," Bluesky said.

"Well, I'll tell you," Westermeyer said, "a theory like that works out fine with respect to the Quantextil who lived in the other villages, and it's the one AnthropoCo settled for, but it comes up slam-bang against the wall with respect to the Quantextil who lived in *this* village. A blight didn't strike *their* wheat. *They* weren't faced with starvation. Why did *they* run off and kill themselves?"

"That's what we're asking you," Bluesky said.

"Did the same blight that killed the wheat kill the other trees too?" Matthews asked.

"According to BotaniCo."

"And yet it spared Kansasia and this tree. . . . I wonder why."

"So does BotaniCo," Westermeyer said.

"Maybe it wasn't a blight. Maybe it was something else."

"Nonsense. It had to be a blight of some kind. What else but a blight could have laid waste to the vegetation of half a continent?"

Westermeyer excused himself, got up, and went to the "wine cellar" for a liter of wine. The cellar was a small storeroom just beyond the kitchen. The hotel had no true cellar, nor did any of the other buildings that comprised the village. Apparently the Quantextil had not believed in cellars, or had never heard of them. Katerina distributed wine glasses and returned to her station in the kitchen doorway. Strong thought he felt her eyes upon him, and he looked over to where she was standing just in time to see her glance away. Beside him, Peake remarked that the shortcake had been good, what there'd been of it. Strong paid no attention. The wine Westermeyer brought back was a deep, clear crimson. "From the vineyards of *Planète Paisible*," he observed as he began filling the glasses. Strong turned his upside down. He never touched wine anymore. Not even mild table wine such as this. Once, a long time ago, he had had a thing about Mary Muscatel, but he had severed their relationship one fine day and henceforth had had nothing to do either with her or her cousins.

After Westermeyer sat back down, the conversation drifted to the 3V team that was due to arrive early the next morning. The wine lent Westermeyer a jovial air. "You're going to be a 3V star, Mr. Strong," he said.

"So long as they stay out of the tree," Strong said.

"But they won't. They'll want an on-the-job interview with you."

Strong looked at Matthews. "Matty, you're not going to allow them in the tree, are you? Suppose they got hurt? They could sue you blind, and your insurance company would only laugh."

"Not if they signed a waiver relinquishing the right to make any claims."

"Ban them from the village!"

"They've already got clearance from MOEL." She looked back at Strong. Tenderly. Of her three-man crew, she liked Strong best. She liked Bluesky next best; Peake, she did not like at all. Nevertheless, it was Peake whom the twenty-five-year-old girl imprisoned in her old-woman's body would have gone to bed with. "Tom, you know how those people are. If I stood in their way, they'd walk right over me."

"I don't want them in the tree!"

"Let's let it go for now, Tom. Maybe when they see the tree they'll forget about close-ups. Go to bed and get some rest. It'll be awhile before you get a chance to sleep in a real bed again."

"Sure," Strong said.

"I'm curious about something," Westermeyer said, addressing Matthews. "Obviously you don't have the manpower to put more than one man in a tree at a time, and you and Mr. Strong have already explained how that man is selected. But why does he have to remain in the tree till the actual felling? Why can't he come down at night? Why does he have to stay up there in the branches and sleep with the birds?"

"My insurance provides triple indemnity for whoever does the actual treework. The clause becomes effective the moment he begins a tree and remains in effect till he finishes it, and stipulates that he remain in the tree throughout that time. Ordinarily that doesn't pose much of a problem. Only very rarely have we encountered jobs that required more than a day. The biggest tree we ever felled only took two. We figure four days for this one, but even so, Tom will only have to spend three nights in it, and he'll have a tree tent to sleep in and a portable campfire to keep him warm." She winked at Strong. "And if the Good Fates please, a dryad to keep him company."

"Sure," Strong said.

"Well," said Westermeyer, "it looks like from here on out your middle initial is 'T,' Mr. Strong, with 'T' in this case standing for 'Tree.'"

Strong stood up to go. "It looks that way."

Bluesky had drained his glass twice. Now he refilled it with the remainder of the wine. "My middle initial is 'D,'" he said. "It stands for 'Drunk.'"

Strong's room was on the third and topmost floor. Its only window looked out upon the square on a direct line with the trunk of the tree, and whenever you looked out during the day you were overwhelmed by its hugeness, and no matter how many times you looked, you at first mistook it for a black, convex cliff. At night when you looked out, you were unable to see the trunk until your eyes became accustomed to the darkness, because neither star- nor moonlight reached the square, and the blackness there was barely divisible from the blackness of the bole.

During the day, except for early morning and late afternoon, you received the impression that the light beneath the tree was green, and perhaps it was, perhaps the greenness of the foliage and the greenness of the grass connived to drive true daylight away. Looking out the window of the room, you could not see the foliage or any of the lower branches. Only by lying on your back on the floor and letting your head hang over the sill could you see up into the leaves and the limbs.

Lying there, you could look straight up at the gigantic limb whose endmost burst of foliage twinkled in the sun high above the roof.

Strong had opened the window yesterday when he first entered the room and he had not closed it since. He liked the green smell of the tree, even though it emphasized the tree's oppressive omnipresence. Mingled with the green smell was the lilaclike fragrance of the tree's flowers. He did not know what color they were or what they looked like, but their fragrance reminded him that the season was spring and made the tree seem less hostile.

Although part of the village had been vacated, lights shone in the windows of all the houses. The lights came on at night whether there was anyone home or not and stayed on till dawn; then, if the day was sunny, they went off; however, if the day was gray they muted their radiance and stayed on. The Reapers had never been able to find their source to say nothing of figuring out how to turn them off, so they had installed retractible shields to cover them when it was time to go to bed.

The light in Strong's room was still shielded from last night, but the shield allowed enough radiance to get through for him to see to get undressed and to tell where the bed was, so he did not bother to retract it. The bed was inbuilt, as was the teardrop table beside it. The table seemed to grow out of the floor; the bed was a parterre whose flowers were of the two-dimensional variety that grow on counterpanes. The flowers were blurs as Strong slipped between the fresh-laundered sheets. He lay there in the dimness thinking of Marijane. He didn't want to think of Marijane, but he knew that if he didn't he would think of the tree, and he knew that if he thought of the tree he wouldn't be able to sleep. So he thought of Marijane and the mountainside on Dandelion where they had lived together, and the clear, cold brook and the spuming waterfall, and the mountain meadows. And there was no tree anywhere for as far as he could see. But thinking of Marijane proved to be a mistake, because despite himself he thought the idyll all the way through to its cruel conclusion, and the conclusion jerked him wide awake. He lay there sleepless, listening to the footsteps in the hall as the other climbers came to bed. A long while later he heard other footsteps. Soft ones. He heard them pause. Abruptly he remembered the look he had almost intercepted from Katerina. Were the footsteps hers? He got up and went over to the door and opened it. He stepped out into the hall. Just in time to see Katerina slip into the next room. Peake's. He slunk back to bed. Lying there, he almost vomited. She had been looking at Peake, not him. They always looked at Peake. Would he never learn that simple truth? Well, perhaps he could sleep now. He would pretend he was Peake—that was what he would do. He and Peake had grown up together in Neo Frisco. He and Peake and Peake's brothers. Okay, he thought, I'm Peake. And Katerina is lying here beside me. Yes, beside me . . . He realized he was falling asleep. All right! All right! I'll sleep then. And be damned to all of them. Except Matty. But I'll bet she'd sleep with Peake too, if she was younger. Maybe she wouldn't have to be younger. Maybe . . .

When Westermeyer walked home the village streets were empty. He lived in the part of the village that had not had to be vacated. The big part. He had a hovercar but he seldom used it in the village. Only to go shopping—things like that. The rest of the time, while in town, he walked.

After he got out from underneath the tree street lights illumined his way. The source of their light was no mystery: It came from the oil-generator in the big man-made shed near the village's outskirts. Eventually lights would be placed in the square, but not till after

the tree was gone. The square, without that ghastly
monstrosity of a trunk rising out of it, would make an
ideal park. Get rid of that damned birdbath too!

When he came to his house he saw by its shielded
lights that his wife had gone to bed. She and he had had
two sons: One taught school on Ariadne, and he and
his wife had a daughter. The other—the older one—
was an astronaut on the Chodz-Imperial run. He was
still single. Westermeyer walked right through the house
and let himself out the back door. He wanted to check
on the rotted-out area again to see whether it had gotten worse since he had looked at it this morning. He
had picked up a flashlight on his way through the
kitchen; now he shined the light on the wall next to the
back steps. Probably the area was no worse than it had
been that morning, but in the artificial light it looked
worse. A ragged expanse of rotted wood almost as large
as the trunk cover of Westermeyer's hovercar.

The trouble was, it could not be fixed. Oh, the section could be removed and replaced—it would not be
easy, but it could be done—but whatever wood he
might use to replace it would not glow the way this
wood did, and the perfection of his dwelling would suffer. He could cover the replaced section, of course
. . . but suppose, after he removed the rotted section
and replaced it, the wood continued to rot?

It would not, of course—not when the tree was gone.
Any more than the rotted sections in the other houses
would expand their present boundaries. The tree was
the true villain. His house was east of it, and not long
after noon his house lay in shadow for the remainder of
each day. The houses to the west lay in shadow all
morning. Those to the north lay in shadow too, for
most of the year. Those to the south—well, they knew
uninterrupted sunlight the whole year through, except
when rain or snow was in the offing, or falling. Plains'
axial tilt gave them that. But even some of them were

beginning to rot. It was as if the village had caught a
disease.

Disease, hell! Westermeyer thought. He turned and
faced the tree. It hid half the sky. He stood in star- and
moonlight, for Penelope, the first of Plains' two moons,
was halfway up the slope of the eastern sky. He shook
his fist at the tree. "Damn you!" he whispered. "Damn
you and your infernal shade! I hope you rot in hell!"

II

Yggdrasill astralis
Height: 1041'
Maximum diameter: 48'
Leaves: 4"–6" long by 4"–5" wide. 4–5 lobes
with wide–spaced sharp teeth. Dark green in
color.

PEAKE halted the airhauler directly above the center
of the green cloud of the tree and actuated the sky
hook. The hook shot high into the Van Gogh–blue
morning sky and spread its invisible umbrella-field, sus-
pending the airhauler on a square mile of air. Strong,
holding his acrophobia at bay, stepped down upon the
sack, which Bluesky had already attached to the winch
cable, and Bluesky, at the winch controls, lowered him
into the tree.

A blue eruption of haha birds greeted Strong's entry
into the canopy. They were long, sleek birds with tiny
golden eyes, their wide wingspan indicating the vast
distances they could cover in a single flight. Most had
already left the tree for the day. Those that Strong's
entry had disturbed circled twice around the branches
and reentered the foliage some distance below.

Bluesky continued to lower the sack. Strong tongued
on his lip transmitter. "Take it slow, Owen," he told
Bluesky. "There's more wood down here than there
used to be in the taiga."

19

The hyperbole, while justified, was inapt. The taiga were coniferous, the tree was deciduous. BotaniCo had dug deeply into Scandinavian mythology to find a name for it and its dead companions. Yggdrasill. But the name too was inapt, for the creators of Yggdrasill had visualized it as an evergreen ash. This tree, despite its massiveness, brought the terrestrial hard maple to mind. Certainly its leaves were similar to those of the hard maple. Strong was astonished at how small they were. From the ground they had been indistinguishable, and he had assumed their size would be commensurate with the tree's. It was not. The largest ones were shorter than his hands were long, and not a great deal wider. As he gazed at the leaves he saw his first tree flower. It was like a wildflower found in the woods in spring, tiny and delicate, crimson in hue.

His acrophobia diminished as he descended deeper and deeper into the tree. Sometimes he envied Bluesky, who had no fear whatsoever of height. Like his Iroquois ancestors, he had been born bereft of it. Peake had no such fear either, or if he did, he had never betrayed it. But then, Strong had never betrayed his either. Yet it was there, and he always had to fight it whenever he began a tree, and in this tree he would have to fight it four days running. As a treeman, he had been fighting it for years. If you added his boyhood and young manhood, he had been fighting it even longer. As a boy and even as a young man he used to climb trees in defiance of his acrophobia. He did all sorts of derring-do in those days to show that he wasn't afraid of anything, and all the time he was. In school, to conquer his lack of self-confidence, he'd gone out for wrestling, and he'd taken the division title in his weight class—the upper middle—two years running and had won a scholarship. His father had laughed at him and said, "Hell, if you could somehow throw your shadow you'd still be scared shitless of it!" But his father had been wrong. It wasn't his shadow that frightened him, it was himself. His eternal doubt that he could not do something as well as it should be done.

He passed the first major bifurcation. It provided the tree with two crests, which meant it would have to be topped twice. He went on down. He had to straightarm some of the limbs, and his descent grew ever more difficult as the limbs gradually grew greater in girth. He thought of the understory. The limbs there were like horizontal sequoias.

Bluesky's voice sounded in the tiny receiver attached to Strong's left ear: "How's it down there, Tom?"

Strong tongued on his transmitter. "Cool."

It *was* cool. Partly because next to no sunlight got this far down in the tree, mostly because of the tree's transpiration. Cool and green. But not quiet. His descent kept disturbing bevies of haha birds, and they kept winging away from his alienness. The call that lent them their name (OrnithiCo had despaired of finding a more appropriate one) seemed derogatory to the human hearer, but the birds had no real awareness of such hearers. Many of the birds he saw could barely fly. Fledglings. The nests they had so recently vacated were everywhere. The birds that had left the tree for the fields (he assumed) were the hunters and the huntresses. No one knew, not even OrnithiCo, whose study had been aborted when the Co-op arrived, what they foraged for or what they brought back for the other birds to eat. And no one cared.

When Strong estimated he was one-third of the way down, he told Bluesky to halt the winch. Then he secured the sack clamps to a limb wide enough to camp on. Opening the sack, he withdrew his saddle rope and hung it over his shoulder. His lightweight beamsaw was already attached to his belt, as were his safety rope and his canteen. He had affixed the long spurs to his boots before leaving the airhauler. Wedging his left foot in the hook that had held the sack and crooking his left arm around the winch rope, he said, "Up, Owen," into his transmitter and began the return journey.

The way back always seems shorter than the way to. This is true of vertical as well as horizontal distances. But it did not prove to be true for Strong in the present instance. The ascent had barely begun when Matthews's voice sounded in Strong's left ear. "Tom? . . . Matthews here. I overslept. Everything okay?"

"Everything's fine, Matty."

She was calling from the hotel dining room where she had set up her screens. There were three of them, each attuned to a camera in the airhauler, but although, like Peake and Bluesky, she could see the top of the tree, she could not see into it. "Hell of a day to oversleep," she said.

"I'm on my way to the first cut."

"Fine. Keep me posted."

"Will do."

Strong concentrated on the sights and smells around him. He gazed at green bursts of leaves and breathed the fragrance of the crimson tree flowers. He looked at intricate arabesques of sunlight. He had to kick away from some limbs and straightarm others. At length he came to a "clearing" and, taking advantage of the freedom it afforded him, lit a cigarette. As he did so, his gaze touched a burst of foliage high above his head, and he saw what he thought was a dryad.

Dryads were to treemen what mermaids, once upon a long time ago, had been to sailors: a myth that everyone made fun of but that everyone—if he happened to be a treeman—secretly hoped was true. A joke tossed back and forth to chase away loneliness and sometimes desperation. You didn't believe there were such beings, you told yourself; you knew damn well that no matter what tree you climbed on whatever planet, no ethereal lady elf was going to beckon to you from some leaf-trellised boudoir and dare you to come and get her. Yet all the while you were telling yourself one wouldn't, you kept hoping that someday one would.

Particularly if you were a treeman like Strong.

He and Bluesky and Peake had tossed the joke back and forth, with Matthews sometimes intercalating a wry comment, all the way through overspace from Chodz, where they'd felled a stand of voracious *currah* trees, to Plains. There had to be, the three men kept telling each other, at least *one* dryad living in the last Yggdrasill on the fifth world of Genji. And oh what a time whoever drew the long blade of grass was going to have after he caught her.

All right, Strong told himself. You saw her. Now let's see you catch her.

It had been the most evanescent of glimpses—a hint of curves and color, a seeming burst of sun-gold hair—and as the image faded from his retinas the conviction that he had seen anything at all faded from his mind. By the time the winch cable brought him to the bower where he thought she had been, he was positive she would not be there. Nor was she.

He saw that his hands were trembling, that the cigarette he had lighted had fallen from his fingers. He was furious with himself. It was one thing to joke about dryads, it was quite another to interpret a prankish play of sunlight on leaf and limb as a manifestation of one. Had his flight from Marijane also been a flight from the whole world? And had it taken him so far afield he could no longer distinguish between illusion and reality?

Angrily he routed the dryad from his mind and fixed his attention on his ascent.

Then, not far down from the crest, he saw her again.

She seemed to be leaning against the trunk, her long legs braced on the limb he had just come even with. Tenuous of figure, vague of face, sunny of hair. His descent and ascent had been and were being conducted a considerable distance from the tree's bole, but she couldn't have been more than twenty feet away.

He closed his eyes and opened them. She was still there. He tongued on his transmitter. "Hold it," he told Bluesky.

When the winch stopped, he stepped off the hook and walked toward her along the limb, his acrophobia completely forgotten. She did not move. Again he closed his eyes and opened them. She went right on standing there, her back pressed against the trunk, her long legs slanting down to the limb; immobile, statuesque. She was wearing a short tunic woven of leaves that matched the tree's. Sandals, also woven of leaves, were interlaced halfway to her calves. Her sunny hair fell all the way to her shoulders. Her features were small but not pixyish. Her eyes were a bright blue. She was utterly beautiful. She was the most beautiful woman he had ever seen in his whole life.

He was so close to her now that he could have reached out and touched her. He started to. The second he raised his arm, she twinkled out of sight.

Twinkled. There was no other word for it. She did not walk away or run away or fly away. In the strict sense of the word, she did not even disappear. She simply twinkled from view.

Bluesky's voice: "Everything okay down there, Tom?"

Strong pulled out his handkerchief and wiped his face. He took a step backward. Another, balancing himself without conscious effort. The dryad did not rematerialize. There was a small cluster of leaves where she had stood, a patch of morning sunshine.

"Tom?"

"Everything's fine, Owen. Just doing a little reconnoitering is all."

"How's she look?"

"She—" He realized just in time that Bluesky was referring to the tree. He wiped his face again, wadded up the handkerchief, and shoved it back into his back pocket. "She's big," he said. He turned, and after covering the remaining distance to the winch cable and relocking his left foot in it and crooking his left arm around the cable, said, "Ready when you are, Owen."

He was still shaken when he reached the crest he had left both a short and a long time ago. Although there were two crests, he could not see the other because of the obscuring branches and leaves. He stepped off the hook and braced himself in the topmost crotch—or at least the highest one that would support his weight— and while Bluesky retracted the cable and attached the tongs, he looked through the interstices of the leaves and the branches at that part of the Plains landscape that was visible to him, hoping to redirect his thoughts into safer channels.

He could not see any of the other trees—the dead ones that still stood like sentinels in the centers of their vast, basinlike wastelands—nor had he expected to. The nearest was at least three hundred miles away. He could remember them, though—remember how tiny they had appeared in the viewplates of the shuttleship during descent, leafless twigs standing like dead sentinels under Genji the sun. There were a dozen of them altogether, if he remembered right: a dozen ghosts guarding decayed villages that had been invisible in the viewplates. He would not even have known the villages were there had not he read the part of the Plains directory that dealt with New America.

Blight?

Perhaps. But what manner of blight killed wheat and houses and trees?

Plains wheat—more specifically, New American wheat—was dark gold in color when viewed from a distance. Thus the wheat that encompassed Bigtree was like a dark-gold sea. A dark-gold sea that rippled in gentle waves in the morning breeze; a sea that seemingly had no farther shore. The basin effect detected by the planetologists was not visible: It was so slight that only the specialized instruments the planetologists employed could detect it. Thus the sea Strong saw from the tree seemed to spread out evenly for as far as he could see. It was not a sea you could drown in, but it was one you could become lost in when the stalks of wheat matured, for at maturity they were higher than a tall man's head. They were not mature yet, but they would be in another two months. The Reapers could then harvest their first crop of the year.

Strong's angle of view was such that the lower stories of the tree hid all but the outermost houses of the village. It was not a large village. None of the villages abandoned by the Quantextil had been large. All were of identical architecture. It was difficult to believe that such villages could be the handiwork of mere mortals. It was as though some long-ago pagan god had appeared in the Plains sky and said, "Let there be houses!" and the houses had appeared. And it was as if that same god, long afterward and perhaps offended by the conduct of his children and jealous perhaps because the houses he had created were as immortal as he, had reappeared and said, "Let there be great trees growing in the midst of the villages so that the houses I have wrought will rot in their shade and transpiration!"

And apparently it had been so.

The chinooklike wind that made it possible for the Reapers to plant an early wheat crop breathed across the plain from the west and rippled Strong's thinning hair. His angle of vision permitted him to see the big sheds (one of which had been partially emptied to accommodate the airhauler) that housed part of Kansasia's planting and harvesting equipment. Other such sheds, scattered throughout the rest of the territory, housed similar equipment, but the nearest was beyond the horizon. Near the local sheds stood the brand-new sewage incinerator with which the Reapers had supplanted the primitive incinerator built by the Quantextil. He could also see the new crematory. (The Quantextil crematory, Westermeyer had said, had been offensive to the eye; the Reapers' had a slight dash of the Parthenon about it.) The foliage of the tree hid the new processing mill the Reapers had built to take care of the forthcoming wood and obscured the distant grain silos where the wheat was stored until shipment.

The tongs were on their way down—the smallest of the three pairs, but huge in their own right. They halted midway between the airhauler and the treetop as Matthews's voice came over the air. "All right, you guys—come on down. You too, Tom. Leave your gear in the tree."

Peake's voice: "What gives?"

"An injunction. Seven Hundred Wonders got one in the Helisport court ordering the felling stopped. Westermeyer just told me. But he says it'll be overruled by tonight and we can start again tomorrow morning. Tom?"

"Here, Matty."

"I've got some news you may or may not be interested in hearing. But I thought I'd better pass it on. Remember the 3V girl you went with on Dandelion?"

". . . I remember." Matthews didn't need to say more. Strong knew what was coming next. And he was sick.

"Well, she got this assignment too. She just came in with two cameramen. The cameramen aren't the ones she was with on Dandelion. They're new."

"Oh," Strong said.

"I thought I'd let you know."

"Thanks, Matty."

* * *

Matthews laid down her transmitter in front of the
center 3V screen. She hadn't wanted to tell him, but
someone had to, so why not her?

He had had a thing about Marijane, Strong had.
Perhaps he still did.

She didn't know what exactly it was he had had, but
knowing Tom, she could guess. To him, women like
Marijane came in big Christmas packages. No matter
how many times you unwrapped the packages to find
their contents came from a secondhand store, you were
always bedazzled by your first sight of them.

Marijane and her two companions had gone upstairs
to their rooms to rest now that they knew they would
have the day off, and except for Westermeyer, Matthews had the downstairs of the hotel all to herself.
After delivering his news, Westermeyer had sat down
not far away in one of the dining-room chairs. He
looked tired. No, not tired—haggard. He wanted the
tree down, and he wanted it down badly. No more so,
perhaps, than the other Reapers, but on him it showed.
He should have been in his office in the municipal
building (a second large building in Bigtree whose original function no one knew) conducting the affairs of the
village. As Co-op head, he was *ex officio* mayor. But
possibly there were no affairs at the moment to conduct. In any case, it was clear to Matthews that, for the
time being, he wasn't going any farther than he had
come.

"Well," she said, "I seem to have gotten up for nothing."

"My house is rotting away," Westermeyer said. "The
whole damn village is rotting away. And those clowns
had the gall to get an injunction!"

Matthews leaned back in her chair. For the day's
work she had donned her usual calf-high boots, denim
breeches, and a plaid shirt. She felt silly sitting there in

front of the three empty screens. "One day shouldn't make any difference," she said.

"It's the idea! Well, thank God the Triumvirate's on our side. I don't think Seven Hundred Wonders realized to what extent."

"Last night you mentioned a feasibility study the Reapers were making," Matthews said. "A study intended to determine whether your wheat can be grown elsewhere. Have you had any success so far, Doctor Westermeyer?"

Westermeyer hesitated, then shook his head. "No. We've a group working on it, but so far they've got nowhere."

"But surely your wheat can be grown elsewhere."

"Can it? If so, we haven't found the right soil. I mean," Westermeyer added, "the right soil and the right climate."

"But surely there are similar soil and climatic conditions on at least one planet."

"No doubt there are. But thus far we haven't run across them, and we have soil samples and meteorological data from almost all the umbilical worlds."

"I see," Matthews said. And she did too, but not in the sense Westermeyer intended. If the wheat the Reapers grew in Kansasia were to be grown elsewhere, its value would depreciate. The Triumvirate, like most governments that had gone before it, had a layer of density impervious to common sense. The last people they should have chosen to make the feasibility study had been the first.

Since Westermeyer gave no indication that he intended to leave, she stood up, at the risk of seeming rude. She didn't feel much like talking, and for the moment at least she didn't feel like talking to a political scientist who had discovered late in life that more money could be obtained from dirt than from his profession. "I hope you'll forgive me, Doctor," she said.

"I've a few things I've got to do, and today seems like a good day to do them."

"Of course, Ms. Matthews." He accompanied her to the dining-room door. "I'll let you know the second we get the okay to resume."

She watched him descend the foyer steps and step out into the morning. Then she climbed the stairs to her room. It was on the third floor, like the others, but it did not face the square. Its single window looked out upon a series of backyards. Such backyards! The lawn furniture cheapened them—yes—but not enough to matter. She looked and she looked at them after she closed her door. Presently she realized she was sitting on her bed with her emptiness.

She got up at once. Do, she thought. Things to do. There wasn't anything she *really* had to do, but there were a number of things she *could* do. She sat down at the little writing table that, like the rest of the room's furniture, grew—or seemed to—out of the floor. She started with the amount she had bid for the tree job and began deducting from it. It was a respectable sum, but the deductions were respectable too. The trip from Chodz to Plains (the trip from Plains to Scanapleton, which was where their next job was, would be deductible from that bid), the treemen's wages, Strong's forthcoming double time, the percentage of the net she'd have to shell out to the External Revenue Service. But even after she finished making the deductions, the amount of money remaining was still a respectable sum. "We're doing all right, Blair," she said to her husband who had come into the room and sat down on a chair that had no more existence than he did. But she realized right away that he wasn't there, no more than the chair was, and remembered that when he died she had hated him almost as much as she now hated the hollowness he had left her with.

He had started out the way Strong and Peake and Bluesky had, as a treeman. But, unlike them, he hadn't been a misfit. The company for which he worked confined its operations to Earth, but he had seen almost at once the possibilities such a business might have were it to be conducted interplanetarily. The concern the peoples of Earth had once felt for their environment had died out long ago, and it had not followed them like a gray ghost to the new worlds the development of the trans-astralis drive had dropped on their collective lap. There were thousands, millions, of trees that would need to be removed, and he, Blair Matthews, the owner of TreeCo, would remove them.

And he had done so—until he died two years ago. And now his wife, Amy Matthews, removed them, employing the same three men he had employed. Oh, she had competition—far more than he had ever had—but she still carried out his dream.

If you could call removing trees a dream.

Certainly it was as much of a dream as cornering a wheat market that might, if elaborated, end once and for all the hunger that still persisted, despite political asseverations to the contrary, both on Earth and on the new worlds.

She realized that she was still sitting there in her chair but that her gaze had moved. Back to the exquisite backyards. She counted them. She could see five altogether. Were she to move closer to the window she would be able to see more. "Christ, I don't want to see backyards!" she said. "My life is a backyard!"

What did she want to see?

The answer, as always, devastated her: Nothing.

She went over to the bed and lay down on it. She had thought running TreeCo would help. It had, to an extent. But she was still empty. Her hollowness lay there with her.

* * *

Life in Bigtree went on as casually as if the tree, upon whose doorstep the Reapers had deposited the blame for the decay of their houses, was not doomed to die. While it was true that word had not yet gotten around to everyone that the removal work for the moment had ceased, the main cause for the present lack of outward interest on the Reapers' part was that air traffic over the village had been prohibited by Westermeyer until the tree was gone, and there was no way yet for the Reapers to watch the devastation that was either being wrought now or that soon would be.

Oh, there were a few curious people standing along the cordoned-off edge of the airhauler route, Peake noted after he left Strong and Bluesky and headed for Katerina's house, but all of them departed after he hollered out several times that the removal was postponed for a day. Most of them were women, some carrying babies. Between planting and harvesting a crop most of the male members of the Co-op spent their time surveying its growth on long Haus Meiten flights and checking for damage from thunderstorms and wind. The Reapers Peake saw were young, which was to be expected since MOEL had used youth as a criterion as well as green thumbs and bright brains, making exceptions in cases like Westermeyer's where leadership and proficiency in a nonagricultural field were required.

Peake had Katerina's street and house number. He had already phoned. She and her husband had separated not long after their arrival on Plains, and he had moved into the Dorm—a house the Reapers reserved for the handful of single men in their group. They had also reserved such a house for the handful of single women who had also been chosen by MOEL, but Katerina, registered with her husband as a house owner and now considered, because of her sex, as its proprietor, had her own "Dorm."

"Gingerbread" was the word Peake thought of when he saw it. It was the wrong word, but it came into his mind when he walked up the corduroy walk to the front door. Katerina met him there. She would be free till eleven, she had told him over the phone. At eleven she would have to go to the hotel. It was not yet nine. Plenty of time. She ushered him into an enchanting living room and, a short while later, into a bedroom that was no less enchanting. "Enchanting" was not Peake's word. He still stuck with "gingerbread."

Since women came easily to Peake, he thought of them as sows, and after one or two encounters he invariably managed to pick a fight with them and free himself. But he wasn't quite ready to pick a fight with Katerina yet. He made a date with her for that night after she finished serving the evening meal at the hotel. It can truly be said that Peake had a function in life, and that he had found it at an early age.

The reason Strong had severed his relationship with Mary Muscatel was that one day after a weekend with her Peake had taken his picture when he wasn't looking, and afterward he stared for a long time at the poor son of a bitch sitting there on the front porch of the inn where they'd been staying on Formidable, stared at the slightly protuberant glassy eyes and the swollen face and the unkempt hair and the filthy clothes, and when the next weekend came around he didn't go near her, and he had had nothing to do with her since. She had amber eyes, Mary Muscatel did, and a slow, steady smile, and when you first met her you thought that here, surely, was the girl you'd been looking for all your life, the girl who would gladly share your dreams; and for a while she did share them, even helped you to dream them. But after a while she got wild and demanding and began to pose problems, not only with herself but with the bottles she came in. What to do with all those damned bottles? And what, in God's name, to do with her?

He wished now, sitting in his hotel room, that he hadn't been so brusque when he abandoned her. It wasn't that he couldn't find her readily enough if he went looking for her; it was just that in abandoning her so brusquely he had done something to himself, cut something out, a malaise of some kind, or a cancer, and because of what he'd done he couldn't go looking for her, couldn't have anything to do with her even if their paths inadvertently crossed. Insofar as Mary Muscatel was concerned, he had cut off his balls.

He spent the rest of the day in his hotel room. He had come here directly after leaving Peake and Bluesky in the airhauler shed. He had his lunch sent up and, that evening, his dinner. Matty brought them. He felt guilty about that. She didn't say anything, though—just put them down and left. He spent the time looking out the window at the tree. Last night he'd thought of Marijane so he wouldn't think of the tree, and now he concentrated on the tree so he wouldn't think of Marijane. It had become the lesser of the two evils. He could cope with the tree, however much he might fear it. But he could not cope with Marijane. Not now—not when he knew that she was there.

But she would not cooperate. Once, when he was thinking of the crest and how he would remove it, she ran naked through his thoughts, her black hair a dancing wake behind her. Another time he happened to glance above the window, and there she was, sitting on the granite shelf beside the mountain waterfall from which she had just emerged, and he again felt the water from her thighs and calves falling upon his face, and when it reached his lips he ran his tongue over them and he again tasted the invitation in its very atoms.

But in large part he was successful in concentrating on the tree. The smell of its leaves and the fragrance of its flowers filled the room, and green thoughts of it kept seeping into his mind of their own accord. He did not think of the dryad, though. He was certain by this time that he had imagined her. Whenever she came into his mind, he concentrated his thoughts on the big, horizontal "sequoias" of the lower limbs that he would have to drop directly into the square for further cutting, since they were far too outsized for even the largest pair of tongs. The tree would provide enough trouble without the added complication of a nonexistent inhabitant. So he thought of the "sequoias" whenever, glancing out on a limb, he saw her sitting there in the sunlight; and sometimes, for a change, he thought of the thousands of haha birds that would soon be wholly evicted. But when he thought of the birds, something went wrong with his resolution to remove the tree, something went wrong with the whole deal, and he would wonder what in the world he was doing there on Plains sitting in a little hotel room looking at a tree he had absolutely nothing against and no sane reason under the sun to remove.

After the sun set and darkness crept into the square and the haha birds settled down for the night, Strong heard a knock on his door, and a moment later it opened and Bluesky, carrying a bottle, came into the room. He sat down beside Strong on the bed and took a swig from the bottle without offering it to Strong. He did not ask Strong why he'd stayed in his room almost all day, he only said, "The 3V team's down in the bar and everybody's wondering where you are," and then he said, "It's on again—the injunction was overruled. Westermeyer just came round and told us."

"So fast?" Strong asked. "I know Westermeyer said it wouldn't be long, but I didn't believe him."

"You can't mess with MOEL," Bluesky said. "They got a finger in every court on every planet, including this one. Matty sent word for you to be ready in the morning."

"I'm ready now," Strong said.

Bluesky upended the bottle again. He felt Strong's eyes upon him in the half darkness and said, "Don't worry about me bumping you with a limb, Tom. I'll be sober by the time we get up there."

"I'm not worried."

"My middle name is 'Drunk' for two reasons," Bluesky said. "One's as phony as a Christmas tree, but it's the one I always blame. According to that one, I get drunk because I can't stand being a part of the same race that almost destroyed my own; can't stand doing to other lands the same things that were done to mine. The other reason's the real one: I can't cope."

"I can't either," Strong said.

"But you can cope enough to get by. Maybe you couldn't before, but now you can. I can't—without a crutch."

Strong was silent. Did he really give the impression to others that he walked without a crutch? He found it hard to believe, that he could walk without betraying his hypothetically wooden legs.

Suddenly Bluesky said, "Marijane's down in the bar. Her and one of her assistants. Almost everybody's there. Peake and Katerina. Even Matty. Westermeyer's tending bar."

Strong didn't say anything. He looked down at his hands. They were lying on his lap, and he could see them quite well in the dim light.

Bluesky said, "Marijane didn't mention your name, but she wants to see you. I could tell. She keeps looking over at the door, hoping you'll walk in."

Strong still didn't say anything.

Bluesky stood up. "I just thought I'd tell you. I don't know what happened between you. It's none of my business. See you tomorrow, Tom."

"Sure."

After Bluesky had gone Strong continued to sit on

the bed, looking down at his hands. There was no blood on them. The blood was on her hands. Or was it? Perhaps it was on neither of their hands. Perhaps what had happened had been meant to happen. Perhaps it had been in her genes for it to happen. Perhaps in his.

Gradually he became aware of the tree again. He had never really ceased being aware of it, but for a little while the awareness had been tucked away in a corner of his mind. Now it came to the fore again, and he was glad because it drove away Marijane. He breathed deeply of the tree's fragrance. Oddly, it made him think of a woman's, or perhaps not oddly, for the tree, according to BotaniCo, was female.

He lay back on the bed with his clothes and his tree-boots still on. The walls of his room—the walls of all the rooms in all the village—were almost soundproof, and he could hear none of the sounds that must be coming from the bar. He could hear nothing at all except the sound of his breathing. He gazed at the square of the window, but it was completely black—black with the tree and the night. Penelope, the earlier of Plains' two moons, should be rising by now, and he knew that if he continued to look long enough he would see her light, for a little while, beneath the tree. The tree was one with the night, one with the ambience. He still feared it, yet oddly, as he breathed its leaf smell and its flower fragrance, he felt its branches enfolding him, cradling him, protecting him from harm.

He must have closed his eyes, for when he opened them he saw that there was someone sitting sideways in the open window. A woman. At first he thought she was Marijane, even though he knew that Marijane would never come to him, and then he saw that even in the shielded light the woman's hair held particles of the sun.

He sat up in bed. He could not see her clearly, but she seemed to be dressed the same way she had been dressed in the tree—in a tunic woven of leaves and in sandals similarly woven that were laced halfway to her calves. Her beauty penetrated the dimness of the light.

The room was small, and if he had placed one hand on the floor he could have stretched out far enough to touch her. But he didn't. Instead he sat there in his bed waiting for her to twinkle out of sight. But she did not. At last he said, without hearing his voice, *I really did see you, didn't I? You were there among the leaves when I looked up, weren't you? And, later, you were leaning against the trunk.*

In a way, she said. *In a way, I was.*

Do you live in the tree? he asked.

In a way, she said. *In a way, I do.* And then: *Why do Earthmen kill trees?*

For all sorts of reasons, he answered. *Because they grow on land we want to till. Because they get in the way of roads. Because they stand sometimes where we want to build a house.* And then he realized that she wanted a subjective answer, wanted to know why Bluesky killed them, why Peake killed them, why he, Strong, killed them, and he remembered what Bluesky had said about raping lands and he remembered reading about the concern for the environment that had characterized the latter years of the twentieth century, only to be forgotten the moment trans-astralis opened the planetary frontiers, and he said, *If you're Bluesky you kill them because your genetic disdain for height makes felling them a logical occupation. If you're Peake you kill them because such a job affords travel from planet to planet and from woman to woman, and makes it unnecessary for you to grow up.*

And if you're you?

He found that he could not lie. *You kill them because you're acrophobic,* he said. *Because overcoming your fear of height each time you climb a tree lends you the illusion that you have overcome all your fears. You kill them to bolster a condition contrary to fact.*

Take us the Earthmen, the little Earthmen, that spoil the vineyard, she said, *for our vineyards are in blossom.*

You stole that from my mind, he said. *But you said it wrong. It's "foxes," not "Earthmen."*

Foxes take from vineyards only what they need, and always give it back. I said it right.

Yes, he said, *you said it right.*

I must go now. I must prepare for tomorrow.

I'm sorry, he said. *I'm sorry about the tree.*

I know, she said. *But the part of you that's sorry lives only in the night. It dies with every dawn.*

No, he said, *it won't die.*

But it will, she said. *In the morning you'll think you dreamed me. . . . Go back to sleep, little Earthman. Draw your dreams around you and lie back in your warm, snug bed. Cuddle up with your lies and illusions—*

Sleep. . . .

III

Yggdrasill astralis
Flowers: Exceedingly small, vivid crimson in
color. Each contains a single pistil but no sta-
mens. The arrangement of the petals brings to
mind a tiny chalice.

IN the hotel dining hall Matthews watched the out-
of-bounds houses of Bigtree drift by beneath the airhauler, and presently she found herself looking down at
the top of the tree. She had not overslept this morning.
A cup half full of coffee stood next to her forearm on her
makeshift desk.

The sky above the tree had another craft in it—the
Haus Meiten the 3V team had rented from the Co-op.
She couldn't see it on any of her screens but she could
hear the whine of its motor above the smooth hum of
the airhauler's. Marijane and her two cameramen. They
wanted to get footage on what their late arrival had
caused them to miss out on yesterday—Tom's descent
into the tree. Westermeyer had granted them aerial
rights. She herself, when Marijane agreed to sign a waiver, had agreed to allow them to enter the tree tomorrow afternoon, by which time Tom should have it down
to the understory. She hadn't told Tom yet. She would
wait till after he got into action. She didn't want the
3Vers in the tree any more than he did, but she knew of
no way she could keep them out, other than by sum-

moning the provincial sheriff from Ottowatomy, the nearest settlement to Bigtree, and this she was reluctant to do. She didn't like Marijane. She hadn't liked her on Dandelion and she didn't like her now; but the main reason she didn't want the 3Vers in the tree was that Tom didn't.

Two of the airhauler's 3V cameras faced straight down; the third was positioned so that Bluesky could adjust it to face in any direction she wished to see. Right now it faced the winch section of the airhauler. The pictures in all three screens wavered when Peake launched the air hook, then steadied again. Looking into the third screen, Matthews watched Strong getting ready for the descent into the tree—a simple matter, since he'd left most of his equipment in the branches yesterday. She watched him step onto the steel triangle, seat himself, and watched Bluesky lower him out of range. She picked him up in one of the other two screens then. Was he afraid? she wondered. She always suspected he might be, although he never showed his fear. She saw the blue eruption of haha birds that greeted his entry into the canopy. Well, it's all yours now, Tom, she thought.

Strong had again alternated his thoughts. He was thinking of Marijane now so that he wouldn't think of his acrophobia. Thinking of when he had met her. It was at a dance on Dandelion, and she was dancing with one of her cameramen. One of her studs. The word made him wince even now, but it was the right word and it made him forget, for a while at least, his acrophobia. He hadn't known then, of course, what she was, he hadn't even known she was a 3V reporter and that the man she was dancing with was one of her cameramen.

Anyway, she was dancing, and at length, when the dance ended, he left his place by the wall and walked over to where she was standing at the bar and asked her to dance with him, and she said yes. Just looking at her had been enough to tell him she'd been around. Not that she looked hard—far from it. With her long, black hair, her far-apart hazel eyes, and her high cheekbones, she looked like a young and extremely efficient businesswoman who kicked off once in a while, but not too often, and who would, someday, make some lucky man a fine wife.

When they danced and introduced themselves she told him what she did and mentioned that she was a native of Earth. So was he, and he said so, and their mutual provenance should have gotten their relationship off to a good start, since on most of the umbilical planets natives of Earth were few and far between. But it hadn't. Instead, after dancing with him once she ignored him for the rest of the evening.

At the time he thought, Well, I'm a lousy dancer—what did I expect?

Dandelion was mostly country, but the dance hadn't been a country dance. It had been a siggo, and it had been held in the firehall of Honeywell, a modest-sized city in a broad mountain valley. The third-generation children of the Earth peoples who had migrated to the planet were updated day and night via transastralis 3V as to the *au courant* activities on the matrix world, and were as conversant with the latest dance steps as their remote compeers.

Strong watched Marijane pass from partner to partner the whole evening through, studying her legs when her scarlet skirt whirled above her knees, enchanted by the glimpses he caught of her thighs. They were too large for the rest of her, he thought then (and found out later); but you had to look hard to notice. Practically every man there danced with her at least once. Peake danced with her three times. But Strong, when she continued to ignore him, stayed away. He was still Thomas Strong, subservient only to the same aspects of reality that had brought him through the door, and this was far from the first time he had been defeated. Thus he could accept defeat with equanimity.

The time of the year was late spring, and the dandelionlike flowers that grew riotously upon the lower mountainsides in the planet's north temperate zone and that lent the planet its name were in full bloom. But despite their dandelionlike appearance, they were a far cry from the dandelions of Earth. They would bloom till late summer, and the valley was sweet with their scent, even though now they were closed for the night. It was the sweetness of jasmine and it filled the city of Honeywell. The mountains were veined with silver, though—not gold, as the flowers might have led one to suspect. The colonists who had come to transfer the silver to its rightful place in the umbilical economy had settled in valleys like this one, and the villages in the valleys had grown into small cities. The trees endemic to the region provided the cities with both scenic beauty and shade, but unfortunately a mutation of Dutch elm disease, which had also come to Dandelion, had found some of them to their liking. Enter TreeCo.

Strong lingered in the dance hall till the last siggo was over, and he watched Marijane leave with the cameraman he had first seen her dancing with. Outside he watched them drive off in a hovercar with sequential taillights. The lights left afterimages on his retinas. But he was still Thomas Strong, subservient only to the same aspects of reality that had brought him out that night, and capable of laughing at defeat. The next time he saw her she was lying on her back in an alley next to the Honeywell hotel where she and her two helpers and Strong and the tree crew were staying. Her face was in a shaft of light and he'd had no trouble recognizing her. He assumed her lover was the same cameraman he'd seen her dancing with. Only weeks later did she tell him, quite by accident, that it had been Peake, and by then it was much too late. The metamorphosis the sight of her *in flagrante delicto* had effected had matured into love.

Strong found the crotch in the crest where he had cached his saddle rope, swung himself over to it, stepped into it and told Bluesky to retract the cable and attach the tongs. He looped the rope a short distance out on one of the crotch's limbs, brought it back and tied a double bowline, and slipped his legs through the saddle. With the slack left over from the knot he tied a tautline hitch round the opposite strand; then he sat back in the saddle and by applying pressure to the top of the hitch began descending. One third of the way down the crest, he halted, and when the tongs arrived, he affixed them to the trunk. He had Bluesky take up on the cable till the tongs' teeth bit into the bark, then he descended to the major bifurcation.

By now his acrophobia was forgotten. He stood up in the crotch, untied the tautline hitch, stepped out of the saddle and pulled the rope down and recoiled it. Braced there, he detached his beamsaw from his belt and looked back up the way he had come. He could see past the tongs almost to the top of the crest. Someone was sitting up there among the leaves, someone dressed in leaves that matched the tree's, someone with sun-bright hair and sun-kissed legs. The dream—if dream it had been—that he had meticulously suppressed till now ran through his mind, and once again he saw her sitting on the sill in the window of his room, much the way she sat now on some lofty little limb, and listened to her every word. . . .

Bluesky's voice: "Something wrong down there, Tom?"

Sweat that could only partially be attributed to the minor exertion he had thus far expended had run down from Strong's forehead into his eyes, blurring them. He wiped them on the sleeve of his shirt. He still saw the dryad. He wiped his eyes again. He still saw her. He waved to her, feeling like a fool. She did not move. He waved again. Still she did not move. He made certain his transmitter was tongued off, then he shouted, "Get out of there!" If she heard him, she gave no sign.

A pattern, he thought. I'm seeing a pattern of light and leaves.

Perhaps. But the pattern refused to go away.

Listen, Strong told himself. You've climbed hundreds of trees. Thousands. And there wasn't a dryad in any of them. Not a single one. You made this one up, and after you made her up you dreamed her. There's no more dryad up there than there's champagne in your canteen!

He dragged his gaze down the trunk and positioned himself so he could cut the crest trunk from the outside. He had turned the beamsaw's intensity to *Low* before leaving the airhauler; all he had to do now was point the pinpoint muzzle and depress the actuator. Do it! he told himself. Do it! He closed his eyes and brought his thumb down on the little knob, and when he opened them the XI gamma 16 particles of the beam were eating into the bark and the bast and the xylem. He moved the invisible beam to the left and then to the right. He tongued on his transmitter. "Tension!" he said, and almost instantly the slightly slanting trunk crepitated and grew straight. He repositioned himself and attacked its other side. When it teetered, he said, "Up!" and the crest lifted out of the tree.

There was a downfall of tree-flower petals. One of them alighted on his arm after he stood back up in the crotch, and it looked like a drop of blood. He stared at it in horror, then wiped it away wildly. As the crest continued to rise a sun-filled orifice took its place. Bluesky brought the crest almost to the airhauler's ventral hull, then Peake moved the craft off toward the processing mill, riding easily on his square mile of air. Strong stood in the middle of the orifice all alone staring at the dwindling crest. But he saw no sign of the dryad.

Naturally he didn't. There had never been one to see.

He found the sunlight reassuring, but he did not remain in it for long. By the time the airhauler got back he was positioned in the other crest, ready to affix the tongs. After affixing them he descended back down to the crotch, but this time he did not look aloft before he made the cut. The airhauler bore the second trunk section off, leaving an even larger aperture in the canopy. He got his first glimpse of the Haus Meiten then. It was one of the craft the Reapers used in ferrying themselves from machine shed to machine shed during planting and harvesting, and for reconnaissance, and except for its lack of a rotor it brought to mind an ancient helicopter. As Strong stared at it, it zoomed down for a closer look at him, and he could see its three occupants through its transparent cockpit walls. A woman and two men. They had installed their cameras on the craft's hull and he was in the range of at least two of them. The woman was looking straight at him, as if the lenses of her eyes were cameras too. She had long, black hair and high, wide cheekbones. He twisted around in the crotch and looked in the opposite direction, and a moment later the crescendoing whine of the Haus Meiten's motor took on a softer note as the craft zoomed back up into the sky.

Standing there in the crotch, sweating, he saw that another tree-flower petal had alighted on his shirt. Again he thought, *Blood*, and wiped it away.

"Tom?"

It was Matty's voice. He tongued on his transmitter. "Yes, Matty?"

"Tom, I told them not to zoom you."

"It's all right."

"Tomorrow afternoon two of them are going to descend into the tree."

"I told you I don't want them up here!"

"Tomorrow afternoon I figure you'll have cut down far enough for them to be able to rig up one of their cameras on a limb. Barring bad weather."

"Tell them to go home!"

"Tom, what could I do? Marijane's going to sign a waiver. Christ, Tom, I don't own the tree. All she wants is a brief interview."

Strong fell silent.

Scene: A cabin on a mountainside. *Dramatis personae:* A black-haired girl sitting on the porch steps smoking a cigarette. A man standing in the afternoon shadow of the porch roof just behind her.

SHE: You knew what I was. I never pretended to be anything else. And you said it was all right. Why isn't it all right now?

HE: You know why.

SHE: Because of Peake? Is that what you're trying to tell me? Because of Peake?

HE: Because of him.

SHE: It was all right for someone else to be screwing me, but not him. Is that all it adds up to, Tom?

HE: That's all. But it's enough. We grew up together, Peake and I did. Peake and I and his brothers. I never had a woman he or one of his brothers didn't have first. With me, it was always seconds. Or thirds or fourths. . . . I thought you were the first one.

SHE: My God—what do you want me to do? Unscrew him?

HE: Would you if you could?

SHE: I don't know.

"Tom?"

"Yes, Matty."

"A point I should have mentioned before—and
didn't. Publicity like this'll be a shot in the arm for
TreeCo. Me, I'm too old to care very much, but for you
guys it could mean more money. What do you say,
Tom?"

". . . All right."

"Fine. What do you want for dinner tonight?"

"Whatever you people have."

"I'll get yours ahead of time and have Jake and
Owen lower it to you."

"Whatever," Strong said.

"Finis and out."

In the Haus Meiten, Dastard, who was piloting, said,
"You see that son of a bitch turn his back on us, Marijane? What's with him?"

"I don't know," Marijane lied.

Pruitt, who was working the cameras, said, "He
looked at you like he knows you."

"We had a thing once."

"Oh."

She looked down through the transparent cockpit
floor at the tree, checked the screen attuned to the ventral camera. Strong was in the exact center of it. She
had good help. "Keep him there, Jerry," she told Pruitt.
"Midship."

"Right."

Dastard had to move the Haus Meiten upon the airhauler's return, but Pruitt still managed to keep Strong
centered. Then Strong disappeared into the foliage.
"He's probably going to start on the limbs now," she
told Pruitt. "Catch the tongs."

She kept staring down at where Strong had been. At
the empty bifurcation. She remembered how when he
shaved he let his sideburns grow down to his cheekbones. She couldn't remember from the close-up
whether he still did or not. She would check the tapes

to see. Then, inwardly, she shook her head. No, she would not check them. How he wore his hair was his business—not hers.

Pruitt was standing close to her in the cockpit. They were lovers, she and he. He was a lot like Strong. Always there at her elbow when there was no need for him to be. Protecting her—no, not her: himself—from the semen-filled savages that he eternally imagined wanted to bear her away.

I seem to attract the Jerrys and the Toms, she thought.

And the Johnny Boys, too.

Johnny Boy Dastard was much like Peake, except that he was patient with regard to coital conquest whereas Peake was not. Johnny Boy knew that if he waited long enough he would get to her, and she knew it too. He had already bumbled in on her and Jerry in freefall on the way to Plains. "Bumbled" had been his word when he apologized. The liar! He'd known what was going on before he opened her cabin door.

Still staring down at where Strong had been, she felt slightly sick to her stomach. It wasn't air sickness, and all she'd had for breakfast was coffee, and coffee never make her sick. What made her sick were her thoughts. Her cold calculations as to who was going to get into her next.

She had been brought up a neo-Catholic. Neo-Catholics were the renegades or, rather, the descendants of them, who had severed all conventional connections with the Church when at last a Pope who endorsed birth control had been elected. Their ranks had multiplied over the years, and they were mighty now, and even though the development of the transastralis drive and the colonizing of the umbilical planets had buried the need for birth control as deeply as it had buried concern for the environment and taken it off the lists of state and church responsibilities, the followers of the new Church still periodically marched in the streets of Earth's major Christian cities, stamping their Right to Life staffs, cursing long-dead Pope Leverne-Pierre and damning at the tops of their voices all Christian citizens of the Triumvirate who still persisted in the practice of the pill, the condom, and the I.U.D.

Upon Marijane's menarche her mother had cornered her in the bathroom of the narrow three-storied module house Marijane shared with her parents, her seven brothers and six sisters, and had stockaded the sex education she had received in private school with the neo-Catholic facts of life. (1) A woman's sex system had but one purpose: procreation. (2) Use of any aspect of that system for mere pleasure constituted self-excommunication. (3) Adultery, as defined by the neo-Catholic Church, referred not only to the transgression but also to the use of devices and/or drugs, whether or not the users were married to each other. And (4) Abortion could be atoned for only by submitting oneself to a clitoridectomy.

Marijane hadn't believed number four, but it had terrified her just the same. She lived in the stockade till she was eighteen, and when she went to college she was a virgin. "You're pure," her father had told her. "As pure as the wind-driven snow." In fact he had thought she was so pure that he let her attend a non-neo-Catholic college. But she hadn't been pure in her mind, she had been frightened. Freed for the first time from her parents, she proceeded to knock the stockade down, except the section that dealt with abortion, and she would have knocked that down too, if it had been necessary. When she went home that summer her father still thought she was pure, and this bothered her to a point where she almost confessed her apostasy to him. Perhaps eventually she would have, but he died during her second year in college. Confessing it to her mother was out of the question. Her mother was pregnant with her fifteenth child. Marijane didn't go home much after that. She had to work evenings and weekends and all summer to cover her tuition, and she didn't want to go home anyway—she felt like a whore every time she entered the house. And she didn't like any of her brothers or any of her sisters, because all of them really were pure. As soon as she graduated she got a job with Transstar Networks. An errand girl at first, but she learned the rules fast and in no time knew which people to ingratiate herself with and which to walk over and which to knife when they weren't looking, and she got into Trans-Astralis News, and first thing you knew she was off Earth on an assignment. It was a minor assignment, and so were the ones that followed; but gradually they grew. Her name had been Mary Janus. She changed it to Marijane. And she leaped from star to star. From Ariadne to Formidable to Acre in the Sky to Moons' Rest to Lapis Lazuli to Dandelion to Plains. And with every leap she dragged the razed stockade behind her. Worse, her father's booted foot had somehow become caught in the debris, and whenever she leaped she dragged him too.

"Look," Jerry Pruitt said suddenly, "there goes the first limb!"

Strong had disdained cutting the upper limbs—they were much too small to bother with—and the one the airhauler now lifted from the tree was well worth a trip to the mill. He sat back against the trunk and watched the tree-flower petals fall. He was glad he was far enough away so they couldn't fall on him.

The foliage above his head provided a horizontal green curtain, hiding the stage of his endeavors from the occupants of the Haus Meiten. This pleased him. Presently he got up and walked two thirds of the way out on the next limb. He had retied his saddle after looping the rope over the major bifurcation, so he could

not fall far. But falling was a million miles from his
mind. When Bluesky relowered the tongs Strong fed
Peake directions via his transmitter, and when the tongs
were correctly positioned he clamped them in place.
Back to the trunk for the cut. He made the overcut
first, told Bluesky to give him tension, then made the
undercut. Leaning against the trunk, he watched the
second limb vanish from view.

Below him he could hear the haha birds. The few
that still remained in the tree. The rest were far out
over the fields, foraging. The seeming laughter of those
in the tree seemed ridiculous now. So did thoughts of
the dryad. He was a machine now, Strong was. By noon
he had removed a total of eight limbs and was quite
deep in the tree. Bluesky lowered his share of the lunch
the crew had brought: two ham sandwiches and a disposable Thermos of coffee. After eating Strong removed four more limbs, then began removing the de-
nuded trunk, first in thirty, then in twenty-foot sections.
Around five o'clock, when the airhauler returned for
the final section, Bluesky lowered his dinner.

Bluesky also lowered a container of water. Strong
washed on a lofty limb beneath the sky. The airhauler
moved off toward the sheds. The Haus Meiten had already called it a day. Since the sack he'd secured the
preceding morning was still a good twenty feet below
him, he sat down on the limb with his back propped
against the trunk and opened the dinner carton Matty
had sent. The moment he relaxed, he met his fatigue,
and he was glad he could spend the night in the tree, in
his tree tent, by his fire. The meal featured fried
chicken. There were biscuits to go with it, cabbage
salad, and a bowl of peas. And cranberries. Matty knew
how he liked cranberries and had sent up an extra portion. They came from the major continent of Plains'
opposite hemisphere. Its first French settlers had
named it Bijoux because of the numerous blue lakes

that characterized its forested northlands. The indigenes who lived there were as human as those who had lived in New America, further strengthening the Apost-Held theory that eons ago the inhabitable planets of the MWG had been seeded by outsiders.

The water container, the dinner carton and utensils were all disposable. He left them there and went down in his saddle to the limb where he'd secured the sack. The limb was big and broad, ideal for pitching the tree tent. He had it up in no time, the portable campfire positioned before it. He didn't actuate the fire yet—he was still overheated from the day's exertions. The tree was all around him now, above, below, and on either hand, and it was as if he had made no headway at all, as though he hadn't removed so much as a single branch.

"How was the chicken, Tom?"

It was as if Matty were sitting beside him on the limb. He tongued on his transmitter. "Fine," he said.

"I'm still looking forward to mine. I'm at the processing mill. The super called me over. Tom, we seem to be removing a tree that has an abnormally large vascular system. The super wants to know if maybe you noticed."

"No," Strong said. "The beamsaw glazes every cut I make, and burns off the sap in the process."

"Barrows—he's the super—made a cross-grain cut for me with their ice-saw on the last trunk section the hauler brought in. Relatively speaking, the phloem tissue and the xylem, or sapwood, comprise twice the amount of space they do in ordinary trees. Barrows thought I might have encountered trees like this before. I haven't. Have you?"

"No," Strong said. "But I don't think he's got much of a problem. He'll have to kiln the wood longer is all."

"True. It's more of a mystery than a problem. What neither of us can figure out is the reason for so huge a vascular system. Granted, the tree's big, but the girth of its trunk and limbs eliminates any need for extra circulatory cells. And there's an added mystery. Some of the phloem tissue and some of the sapwood are dead, or if not dead, dying. In the case of the sapwood this could be ascribed to its becoming heartwood, except that the dead tissue doesn't border the heartwood the way it should. Maybe you can figure it out, Tom."

"I can see why there might be a larger vascular system," Strong said. "The tree's size. It's true what you said about the girth of the trunk and the limbs, but maybe with a tree this big different rules apply."

"Maybe. But I don't think so. Anyway, Barrows wanted you to know, and I did too. Well, I'm going back for dinner now. Get a good night's sleep, Tom."

"Will do, Matty."

"Finis and out."

Night came early in the tree. The haha birds, some of which had just returned from the plain, chirped in the dark-green gloom, blissfully unaware that today's depredation was but a prelude of more to come. After a while Strong glimpsed a star through an interstice in the foliage overhead and knew that true night had come. He had been sitting there trying to sort out his thoughts, but he had gotten nowhere with them. They were wadded-up letters in a wastebasket. He wished he could burn them, but he could not. There was no way to get them out of the basket, and the basket was himself.

At length Penelope, the first moon, came up. He could not see her, but he could see her light eking down into the tree and turning some of the leaves to silver. He saw that his right arm had also turned to silver, and this amazed him. But it did not remain silver long, for the night grew cool and he withdrew into his tent and actuated the V-Epsilon-22 batteries of the campfire and set the intensity gauge on *Low*; then he sat there in cherry-red solitude, gazing across the fire at the night. He discovered presently that he could see all the way to the end of the limb on which the tent stood, could see it stretching away before him for all the world like a leaf-trellised walkway, could see all the way to the argent burst of foliage at its end. Then he saw her. She was walking toward him in the night. At first he saw her only in fragments—an expanse of leg, a silvery shimmer of arm, an argent blur of face; but as her lofty stroll on the leaf-trellised path brought her nearer, the fragments swam together into the thin, pale loveliness of her, and presently she emerged from the final shadow and sat down across the fire from him. Her hair had captured the light of the moon the way by day it captured the light of the sun.

He said, again without hearing what he said, *I saw you this morning way up among the leaves. Almost at the top of the tree. It was you, wasn't it?*

Yes, she said, *it was me.*

I waved to you, but you didn't wave back. I didn't want you to get hurt. What were you doing way up there?

I was watching you.

Where did you go after I cut the crest? I didn't see you any more.

No. But you're seeing me now.

Yes, I'm seeing you now. Are you a dryad? he asked.

In a way, she said. *In a way, I am.*

We always make jokes about dryads—myself and the other climbers. We always pretend we're going to find one in a tree. But it's funny—it never once occurred to me, and I don't think it ever occurred to Peake or Bluesky either, that people like us are the most logical beings for a dryad to hate.

I don't hate you, she said. *I don't even hate the beings who hired you to do what you're doing. All of you are part of an inevitability.*

But you must hate me. I know how I'd feel if I had a home and somebody came around and started tearing it down. I'd hate whoever it was.

I don't hate you, she said again. *You, or any of the others.*

You should, he said. *Do you live in the tree all alone?*

Yes, I'm all alone.

I'm all alone too, he said.

Not now. You're not alone now.

No. Not now.

Penelope had climbed higher into the sky, and now a silvery shard of light lay upon the dryad's face, and he saw that in the moonlight her eyes were dark blue and that the dark blueness went well with the argent light and that she was as beautiful by night as she was by day. What did a dryad do, he wondered, when her tree died?

She dies too, she answered before he had a chance to ask.

But why? There are other trees. Not like this one, and a long way away. After I fell this tree I'll take you to another, if you like.

It wouldn't work that way, she said.

Were there dryads in the trees that died?

Yes. If you must call them that.

And now all of them are dead?

Since their trees are dead they must be dead too.

Last night I thought I dreamed you, he said. *I was certain I dreamed you till I saw you this morning in the top of the tree.*

And then you rationalized me and thought you dreamed me again.

Yes, he said, *I had to.*

Tomorrow it will be the same way.

No, he said. *I know now that you must be real.*

What you know now has nothing to do with what

you'll know tomorrow. Tomorrow you'll think you dreamed me again. You'll think so because you won't be able to fit me into the little box you think reality comes in.

Perhaps you're right.

I know I'm right, she said. *Tomorrow you'll ask yourself how there can possibly be such a thing as a dryad who speaks Anglo-American in a soundless voice living in the tree you have to fell.*

Come to think of it, how can there be? he said.

There, you see? Morning is far away and already you're beginning not to believe. Beginning to think I'm nothing more than an image you projected in your sleep to ward off your loneliness and the emptiness of the night, to keep the complexities of the past from welling up from your unconscious mind and drowning you in unpleasant dreams.

She got to her feet, and once again her beauty smote him, made him yearn to reach across the cherry-red foil flames of the campfire and touch her flesh. But he could not move his arms. *I will leave you now, little Earthman,* she whispered. *Leave you in your little toy bed in your little toy tent, high, high in the tree. Sleep, little Earthman—*

Sleep . . .

From where he was standing next to Bluesky at the hotel bar, Peake could look into the backbar mirror and see Marijane, who sat several yards down the bar in the company of one of her cameramen. And she, of course, could see him also, and every several minutes their eyes touched in the smooth, clear glass.

Since the mirror did not reflect her drink, and since a barrier comprised of Matthews and Westermeyer and his wife existed between them in the real world, he had to guess what it was. But he didn't have to guess, really, since he knew from Dandelion that she always drank

Magellanic Clouds and there was no reason to suppose that she had switched to something else. He himself was drinking Scotch and soda. One percent Scotch and ninety-nine percent soda. He enjoyed keeping his mind clear when the people around him clouded theirs. It gave him both a morning-after and an immediate advantage. He always knew exactly what he'd said and exactly what everyone else had said. But most of all, he enjoyed people making fools of themselves in his presence because they took it for granted he belonged to the club.

Katerina was tending bar. She looked sharp in the Little Miss Muffet outfit she was wearing. She had the type of body that went well with a short, short dress. Both the bar and the backbar were man-made, and somehow did not match the room, even though shelves above the backbar had been reserved for some of the more interesting Quantextil artifacts. In addition to Katerina and Westermeyer and his wife there were perhaps a dozen other Reapers in the room. Their presence had nothing to do either with the presence of part of the tree crew and part of the 3V team: they were the type of people who would have been in the bar anyway. Peake, who was wise in such matters, had already classified them and he'd been unsurprised to find them typical of bar drinkers everywhere. No matter how meticulously chosen any large group of people might be, it would always contain a certain number of drunks, near-drunks, and "socializers."

Katerina had a bar stool behind the bar and she had placed it so that when she sat down she sat across the bar from Peake. She had a way of crossing her legs that Peake liked, and she sat there now with them crossed that way, her left ankle resting on her right knee, and a fold of buttock fat rimming the stool's edge. But his mind wasn't on her legs, it was on the mirror, and in between reflected glances at Marijane he kept thinking of Marijane and the way she had been on Dandelion before Strong, with his schoolboy maunderings, had lured her on a supposedly permanent basis to his bed.

Katerina said, "You must have overworked your buddy. He's sound asleep."

Peake saw that Bluesky had crossed his forearms on the bar and laid his head on them. "Hell, he's not tired," Peake said. "He's just used to sleeping in bars."

He raised his eyes to the mirror and looked at Marijane, and Marijane looked back at him. "What's so interesting in the mirror?" Katerina asked. "Every time I look at you you're staring into it."

Peake wasn't in the least embarrassed. "A girl I used to know."

"The 3Ver?"

"That's the one."

Katerina's blue eyes had turned into glass. "You're living in the present, not the past. You should be looking at me."

"I am looking at you."

"Only when you're not looking at her."

"It's one of those things," Peake said.

"What things?"

"Things you think are over, but aren't."

Down the bar, a Reaper knocked his glass on the wood. Katerina slid off the stool and went to wait on him. Peake watched her behind as she walked. He sighed. It had been good stuff. He picked up his glass and walked down the bar to where Marijane was sitting and stood next to her. A Magellanic Cloud sat on the bar before her. "Hello, Marijane," he said.

"Stop breathing down the back of my neck," she said to her companion. To Peake: "How are you, Jake?"

"Just fine. You?"

"I'm fine too. I was wondering when you'd remember we used to know each other."

Her voice had the same richness he remembered

from Dandelion. The nature of her eyes had somehow
failed the test of the mirror. He saw now how sharp
they were, how dark and daring. With his own eyes he
traced those high, wide cheekbones that hinted Amerind where no Amerind existed; found her black, half
tumultuous hair and fondled its fall down her back. He
said, "You were the last person I ever thought I'd see
on Plains."

"You weren't thinking clearly then. Did you think
my network would overlook the felling of the biggest
tree since Yggdrasill? They bought exclusive rights to
the tape months ago."

"To me it's just another tree," Peake said.

"What're you talking about?" Marijane's companion
cut in. "It's ten times bigger than any tree that ever
grew—except those dead ones out on the plain."

"Jake, this is Jerry Pruitt," Marijane said. "He's my
head cameraman. Jerry, this is Jake Peake. He's one of
the tree crew. We're old friends."

Pruitt nodded distantly. Peake said, "Hi." The clown
looks a little like Tom, he thought.

Marijane said, "We're going to play the tree up as a
sort of evil force and we're going to play Tom up as a
sort of modern-day Paul Bunyan. . . . How is Tom?"

"The same," Peake said. "Still keeps to himself.
Never says much. You're going to have a hard time
passing *him* off as a Paul Bunyan."

"He's up in the tree now, isn't he?"

"Hell, people like Tom are always up a tree."

"Don't you like him?" Pruitt asked.

Peake shrugged. "About as much as he likes me."

"It's warm in here," Marijane said. "Don't they have
air-conditioning?"

"The way I understand it," Peake said, "they don't
install anything if it involves very much cutting. Isn't
that right, Doctor?" he said to Westermeyer, who was
sitting next to Pruitt.

Westermeyer nodded. "We're a bunch of old women when it comes to our houses. We don't like to deface them in any way whatsoever. Fortunately, there's no need to. They generate heat in winter the same mysterious way they generate light the year round. Air-conditioning wouldn't involve much cutting, of course, but we've never bothered with it because as a rule the warmer months are quite cooperative with human comfort."

"I still think it's too warm in here," Marijane said, looking at Peake.

"Maybe a breath of fresh air," Peake said.

She slid off her bar stool and took his arm. "Sounds like a good idea."

Pruitt looked like a schoolboy whose teacher had slapped him. "Please don't go, Marijane," he whispered.

My God, Peake thought, he really *is* like Tom! He felt someone's gaze burning through the side of his head. He knew it was Katerina's, and didn't look. "Let's go," he said to Marijane, and they walked out of the bar.

The square was off-limits, but Marijane ignored the big sign that said so and led Peake across the grass toward the tree. Lights, most of them shielded, in the windows of the encompassing houses threw a wan radiance upon the grass, and so did the nearer street lights, but the closer you got to the tree the paler the light got till at length it became difficult to see, and there, suddenly before you, was the tree, a black, dendritic cliff, rising sheerly upward to the even blacker sky of its limbs and leaves. "It's awesome, isn't it," Marijane breathed.

"It's just a tree," Peake said.

"What's that black thing over there?"

"That's the birdbath."

"Oh. I remember now. . . . I should think Tom would be frightened, up there in the limbs all alone."

"Being alone is what he likes."

"I found that out the hard way."

"He was gone on you. What went wrong?"

She did not answer. Instead she said, "Do you feel the tree? I can."

"I can smell it."

"That's part of it. The green smell. And the scent of its flowers. But there's a sort of presence too. If AnthropoCo's right about the Quantextil's worshipping it, I can almost see why they did."

"They were a bunch of dumb Druids," Peake said.

"Maybe. But—"

"You didn't get me out here to talk about worshiping trees."

She faced him. Her back was to the trunk and she could see the vague outline of him against the village lights. "You always go straight to the heart of everything, don't you?"

"That's what you like about me, isn't it?"

"One of the things."

"People who beat around the bush beat around it because they're afraid to find out what's in it. Like Tom. If he'd looked into you instead of beating around you like a schoolboy around a maypole he'd have known when he saw me screwing you in that alley we were doing it there because you like to screw in alleys, in ditches, in vacant lots."

"I played it straight with him while we were together," Marijane said. "It's not my fault I'm what I am."

"It was when he found out that he couldn't take it, wasn't it? That he walked out on you?"

"No. It was when I let it slip that it was you he saw with me in the alley. It was *you* he couldn't take."

"Well, I'll be damned!" Peake said.

"You and your brothers. He wasn't looking for a saint. He was simply looking for someone you and they hadn't got to before him. And to make it worse, he fell in love with me when he saw us and thought you were my cameraman. At least that's what he told me, and that's when I let it slip it was you."

"Oh, boy," Peake said. "Well, it's like what my old man used to say. You live long enough and you get to see them all."

He felt her fingers on the buckle of his belt and realized she had sat down on the ground. He sat down beside her. "It's not dirty here," he said.

"Sure, it's dirty," she said, her voice faintly thick now. "Didn't you ever hear of meiofauna, Jake? Of springtails, earwigs, sow-bugs and thrips? Well, the ones here are alien meiofauna, but they do the same things around the bases of trees. They eat dead things and recycle them, and the tree eats what they recycle. It's filthy here, Jake—*filthy*!"

The grass upon which they were sitting was damp. He rolled over on her, pressing her into the soft, dark earth.

IV

Yggdrasill astralis
Fruit: A conical nut, russet in color, 1″–1½″
long. Contains a single elongated seed approxi-
mately ½″ in length. The endosperm is white
and rich in carbohydrates. Nuts fall to the
ground late in autumn.

THE singing of haha birds awakened Strong, and when
he crawled out of his tent he saw blue blurs of them
winging through arboreal archways and green corridors,
through leaf-laced skylights and foliaged windows pink
with dawn's sweet breath. The faraway flights of the
hunters and huntresses had already begun.

There were breakfast pacs in the sack, and vaccans
of coffee. He chose a pac that contained cheeseggs and
ham and drank two vaccans of coffee with his morning
meal. Afterward, his mind still pleasantly blank, he lit
and smoked a cigarette. It wasn't until he stood up on
the limb preparatory to striking the tent that his acrophobia returned and, with it, the dream.

Dream?

He stood there fighting both the acrophobia and the
dryad. He had dreamed her twice now. Surely she must
be something more than an unconscious remembrance
of a pattern of sunlight and leaves. Moreover, he could
remember the dreams almost too well for them to have
been dreams. By now the first dream should have vir-

tually faded from his mind, but it hadn't. He could remember it as vividly as he remembered the second.

But to accord reality to a dream for no other reason than that you could remember it subverted the very reality you accorded. If the dryad was anything more than a remembered play of sunlight on leaves, she was probably a camouflaged version of someone he knew, or had known. His mother? He shook his head. His mother had died the same year she bore him. She had fallen down the stairs of the second-story cold-water flat she and his father had lived in in Neo Frisco. She had been drunk, his father had told him years later. He was inclined to believe this had been true. Living with his father would have been enough to make her drink. His only conscious memory of her was from trigraphs and meant nothing to him; and the few months he had spent in her arms could not have instilled too ineradicable an unconscious recollection. There had been "mothers" after her, of course. Sleazy women he had hated and who had hated him. The dryad could not be a version of one of them.

Could she be Marijane?

He spat the thought. Whoever she might be, assuming she was not herself, she was not Marijane. Or any of the other second, third, fourth and fifth shots he had serenaded with his Victorian violin.

Since he could not cope with her and since, even though he still could not explain her, he didn't believe she was real, he banished the dryad from his thoughts and struck and repacked the tree tent in the sack. He had already deactuated the fire; now he shoved the unit into the sack and resecured the sack to the limb. His saddle rope hung down from above like a superpolypropylene liana, and he began the climb to where he'd left off yesterday, fighting his acrophobia every inch of the way. It was better to fight it than to ward it off with thoughts of Marijane. Dawn had given way to day, and as he ascended, the daylight grew brighter with each burst of foliage he surmounted, and the greenness of the tree's interior less intense, till at last he broke the surface of the leaves. When he climbed onto the stub over which he'd looped the rope, his acrophobia lay below him, lost in the foliage.

He ensconced himself in the crotch formed by the juncture of the stub and trunk and scanned the blue morning sky. No sign as yet of the airhauler. Or of the Haus Meiten either. He had left the Plains watch Matthews had bought him in his room, since in a tree he did not need to know the time; nevertheless, he knew that the airhauler was late. The big branches of the tree angling upward all around him hid both the rising sun and the sea of wheat. The branches made the tree, at this stage of its removal, seem like an open flower, and he was in the flower's center, perched on a grotesque "pistil." But the airhauler, when at last it showed in the sky, was a honeybee come not to pollinate but to destroy.

By the time Peake had halted the airhauler and launched the sky hook Strong was way out on the first limb, the morning wind rippling his thinning hair and swaying the saddle rope, which curved back up to the crotch. Soon he would have to begin using tree pegs. They were employing the medium-sized tongs now. He affixed them when Bluesky sent them down, arranging them so that their long teeth would bite deeply into the limb; then he walked back to the crotch, feeding the rope back through the tautline hitch. He turned the beamsaw indicator from *Low* to *Med*, then made the overcut. The limb creaked as Bluesky took up the slack, and the tongs clanked as the teeth bit into the wood. Before making the undercut, Strong, before he thought, looked out along the limb for as far as the foliage would let him see. But it was all right, for he saw no sign of the dryad. Of course he didn't. It was difficult for the sun to fool him now that he was working on the surface of rather than in the tree.

He should have felt better, and he did in a way, but in part of his mind distress reigned; and when the limb broke free and the tree-flower petals drifted down below him like drops of blood, the distress darkened to despair. He saw that his hands were trembling and realized that the sweat running down from his forehead into his eyes was cold.

What's the matter with me? he thought. It's not her tree. There isn't any her.

When the airhauler returned, he was waiting for it on the next limb and affixed the tongs. They were getting down deep now, and the tree shuddered slightly when the limb let go. More tree-flower petals. More "blood." But it wasn't so bad this time, and Strong knew he could make the day.

All this while he had been half watching the sky for the Haus Meiten. He judged the time to be about eight A.M., but the craft had yet to show. It was about time he heard from Matty, and as the thought crossed his mind, her voice materialized in his left ear: "Good morning, everyone."

Strong heard Peake's "Morning" and Bluesky's "Great day." Then he said "Good morning" himself. "Tomorrow," Matthews said, "I want you, Owen, or you, Jake, to wake me up before you go for the hauler."

"I'll catch you," Bluesky said.

"Where're the 3 Vers?" Strong asked.

"I don't know. I thought they were gone."

"No sign of them up here," Bluesky said.

"Looks like I'm not the only one who oversleeps. Well, they'll be around eventually. Tom, you be ready for them this afternoon. Or did you forget?"

"No. I didn't forget."

"I told them they could have half an hour."

"All right."

"Here they come now. For breakfast. Jake, when they get up there, you watch them—okay? Make sure they give you plenty of room."

"I'll watch."

"Finis and out."

Yesterday, for the convenience of his guests but more for the convenience of Katerina and the chef, Westermeyer had installed an automatic coffee machine and an automatic small-meal dispenser next to the kitchen door. Marijane settled for coffee. So did Pruitt. Dastard bought a cheesegg and bacon pac to go with his. They chose a table in a corner, out of Matthews's earshot. Dastard sat at Marijane's left, Pruitt on her right. Pruitt wasn't speaking to her. He looked like the dog she used to torture when she was a kid.

She lit a cigarette to go with her coffee. Usually Pruitt slept with her. Last night he hadn't, and perhaps that was why she had overslept. She was still shaken from the dream she had awoke from, even though it was an old one—a recurrent dream, her analyst had said—that she had had before. But for all the times she had dreamed it, it had never dug its ghastly fingers as deeply into her mind as this time.

Drinking her coffee, smoking her cigarette, Marijane thought it through. She didn't want to think it through, she didn't want to think of it at all; but the ghastly picture in her mind wouldn't go away.

The dream hadn't changed, except for its greater vividness, since she'd told it to her analyst.

"I am walking across a meadow. It is a large meadow—so large I cannot see what type of terrain surrounds it—and there are lovely multicolored flowers all around me. I am barefoot and whenever I step down I crush some of the flowers underneath my feet. Above me the sky is the blue of June skies in the temperate zones of Earth.

"I keep trying to avoid the flowers with my footsteps, but it is impossible. They are always there beneath my feet and I keep killing them. There is a wind blowing. It must be a north wind, for it is cool. I can feel it against my face, my arms, my legs, my stomach, my breasts. It is at this point in the dream that I realize I am naked.

"While I have been thinking about the flowers, the meadow has subtly turned into a hill, a steep hill that grows steeper with every step I take. Presently it becomes so steep that it is vertical, yet I continue walking up it as though it were flat land. This terrifies me, and I try to stop and return the way I came. But I cannot. The flowers are gone now, and the ground 'beneath' my feet is gray-colored, somehow swollen, and I sink softly into it with each and every step I take. I keep wondering if the meadow I crossed is still beneath me, the meadow with its lovely flowers, but somehow, even though I am unable to turn my head to look, I know that it is gone.

"I climb and I climb. Seemingly the hill has no summit, and yet it must have. It is an exceedingly narrow hill, more of a pillar than a hill. But the truly terrible aspect of what I am doing is not the height I have gained but that I am walking on a vertical surface as easily as though it were horizontal, defying a natural law to which both my body and my mind were subservient. With ever-increasing desperation I want to turn and go back down, but I cannot. The hill, if it is a hill, mesmerizes me, makes it imperative that I reach its summit, yet all the while I keep trying to reach it, I do not want to.

"Suddenly the hill begins to pulse 'beneath' my feet. To throb. My impossible footing becomes precarious. High, high above me there is a great rumbling, and I realize in horror that what I have been climbing is not a

hill but some kind of volcano, that it is now erupting
and that any second hot lava will be pouring out of its
interior. At this point my impossible footing becomes
truly impossible, and I am forced to cling to the perpen-
dicular slope by digging my fingers into its strangely
soft surface. Then, above me, I see the lava, only it is
not lava, it is white, like cream almost, and it is descending the slope in great white waves. I know that
when it reaches me it will overwhelm me and wash my
dead body down the slope, and I begin to scream. It is
at this point in the dream that I awake."

Her analyst, working with his psyche-sensors, had
forced from her unconscious mind in her own words
what the meadow flowers and the hill were. Then, after
reexamining her dossier, he had interpreted the dream.
"You do not want to crush the meadow flowers," he
had said, "because they are the children you have never
borne, but you cannot stop crushing them because in
one sense you have already done so. You fear the mon-
strous penis you are climbing because it signifies the
lifestyle for which you abandoned your church. You
want to stop climbing it, but you cannot, because the
pleasure it also signifies outweighs the fear. Then eruption occurs, and you think you fear for your life. Ac-
tually, you fear one of two things, or both: one, that the
pregnancy you have so irreligiously avoided will occur,
and/or two, the end of your present lifestyle. I think we
can go one step farther, Ms. Janus, and say that this
latter aspect of the dream embodies a wish-fulfillment
element: You are dissatisfied with your lifestyle and
want to end it, even if pregnancy is the only way to do
so. Whichever, now that you understand the dream, you
should dream it no longer."

Liar! Marijane thought, lighting her second cigarette. And yet he hadn't been altogether a liar. Last
night was the first time she'd dreamed the dream since
his interpretation.

"Jerry, dear," she said, "get me another coffee."

Without looking at her and without saying a word, Pruitt got up, walked over to the coffee machine, brought back a cup of coffee and sat back down again. "Thank you, Jerry dear."

Maybe, she thought, my unconscious mind is as cruel and corrupt as my conscious. Maybe, unconsciously, I want to suffer. Maybe that's why I dreamed the dream again.

Or maybe seeing Tom again caused it to reoccur. Maybe back on Dandelion when he asked me to marry him, that was why I almost said yes. I'd stopped dreaming the dream but still it terrified me. Maybe I thought that if I married him and had children like he wanted, the dream would definitely never reoccur.

Scene: A granite shelf by a waterfall on a Dandelion mountainside. *Dramatis personae:* A man and a woman, both naked, lying side by side on a shelf near the tumbling water.

HE: You know what I want, Marijane. I want you to marry me.

SHE: Don't be absurd, Tom.

HE: I want kids. By you.

SHE: You're talking like the hero in an ancient movie.

HE: I don't care. The offer still stands. Will you marry me?

SHE: I—I don't know. I'll think about it.

The moment had said, Say yes, and she almost had. But she hadn't. But she had thought about it. Day and night till—till— She blanked the end of the idyll from her mind.

"Well," Johnny Boy Dastard said, drinking the last of his coffee, "I suppose a late start is better than none."

"Yes," Marijane said, finishing her second cup, "and it's getting later by the second." She looked at Pruitt. "Right, Jerry?"

Pruitt didn't say anything. He simply stood up and started for the door. He'll come around, Marijane thought. "Come on, Johnny Boy," she said.

Matthews watched them walk out. Marijane was wearing a white halter, royal-blue clingpants, and white sandals. The whiteness of the halter made her long hair look blacker. Blacker than black. Bitch! Matthews thought. But it was the twenty-five-year-old girl imprisoned in her body talking, not herself. The twenty-five-year-old girl didn't give a damn about poor Pruitt and far less about poor Strong. The twenty-five-year-old girl thought only of herself, and she was mad because Peake had gone for Marijane last night instead of her. My God! Matthews thought. What are women like me made of? And then she thought of the wry answer she had thought up long ago when she *was* twenty-five: Sugar and Spice and Everything Vice.

But the surface Matthews also disapproved of Marijane's behavior last night. The sick look that had come onto Pruitt's face when Marijane and Peake left the bar still clung to her mind. And the surface Matthews, who disliked Peake, wondered what it was that the man had that men like Strong didn't have, what the strange and mysterious quality was that lured women to his side.

A shit-kicker, that's all he is, she thought. A born bum. A cynical expression of manhood some sardonic god placed among mankind to diminish naïve boobs like Strong and Pruitt.

And to dig the caverns in old women like me deeper.

By noon Strong had removed six more limbs in two sections each and had brought the trunk down to base. After getting a lightweight hammer and a pouch of tree pegs out of the sack, he had sent it back up to the airhauler rather than waste valuable time lowering it deeper and deeper into the tree. The tree was half its original height now, and this afternoon the real work would begin.

When Bluesky lowered his lunch, Strong ate the two Plains-beef sandwiches it comprised and drank the throwaway Thermos of fresh coffee that accompanied it, seated in the tree's highest stub beneath a big spray of foliage. The Haus Meiten had been in the sky since about nine o'clock. It was gone now. He dreaded its return, for when it returned, Marijane would probably descend into the tree.

He had removed another limb when Matthews's voice apprised him Marijane was coming. "Two of them," she said. "Her and one of her cameramen. For God's sake, Tom, make sure they don't fall."

Strong looked at the sunlit limb to which he had just descended. It was a wide promenade surfaced with bark, a walkway whose height was hidden by the foliage beneath it, a walkway that seemingly led to the forest of its own foliage. "They won't fall," he told Matthews. "Unless they're drunk."

He sat down with his back against the trunk to await his visitors. Even at this height, the trunk was huge and its bark was beginning to take on the characteristics of the bark farther down—prominences interspersed with depressions. The prominences were slight now, the depressions shallow; but the prominences would become more and more pronounced as he worked his way down, and the depressions, or troughs, deeper.

Presently he saw the Haus Meiten. Peake had already moved the airhauler well to the west so that the 3Vers' craft would have clear sailing above the tree. To Strong, the Haus Meiten looked like a stub-winged moth with a transparent belly. It seemed to climb higher into the sky as it approached, and it did not begin to descend till it was directly above the tree. Strong

did not move. He was in plain view, and the pilot
should be able to see him. Apparently the pilot did, for
the little craft descended straight toward the limb on
which Strong sat. About twenty feet above the limb it
halted, its belly opened, and a man and a woman came
down to the limb in a descent basket and stepped out,
the man with a tripodic camera over his shoulder. The
basket was withdrawn and the Haus Meiten climbed
high in the sky, and Strong had his first good look at
Marijane since he had walked away from the rented
cabin on the Dandelion mountainside.

The sight of her distressed him, but by now he was a
native of distress.

If she knew acrophobia she hid the acquaintance
well. As the panting of the Haus Meiten's stabilizing
motor died away she walked lightly along the limb to
where Strong was sitting. Behind her, her companion
set up the tripodic camera. "Hello, Tom," she said.

She had donned a different outfit for the interview.
A red-plaid shirt, dark-blue breeches, and knee-high
sado-boots. Except for the higher boots it was similar to
Strong's attire, but his was old whereas hers was brand
new. It could be said that hers went well with her body
while his went well with his beard.

He got to his feet. "How are you?" he said flatly,
looking at her hair.

"I'm fine," she lied. Yes, the sideburns were still
there. "This won't take long. Can you bring your rope
down and coil it round your shoulder?"

"All right," Strong said, and stepped out of the saddle and pulled down the rope and began coiling it. He
was glad she had asked him to because it gave him
something to do, lent him a few minutes in which to get
back his breath, because she had knocked it out the
way she always had. She's a pig, he told himself. She's
Peake's pig. But it didn't do any good.

"Jerry's going to 3V us together," Marijane went on,

"and I'm going to ask you a few questions. I want to put you across as a sort of lone lumberjack who's conquering the tree. You're the hero, the tree's the villain. It *is* a villain, isn't it?"

Strong looped the coiled rope over his left shoulder. "The Reapers think so."

"I don't blame them. Westermeyer showed me some of the houses that're rotting. Anyway, the trunk won't do for background—the viewers may think I conducted the interview on the ground. What we should do is get as far out on the limb as we can. So if you'll lead the way—"

Strong left the trunk and started out on the limb. She followed. When they reached the part where her companion was adjusting his camera she introduced the two men. "I brought Jerry because he says height doesn't bother him," she said. Looking into Pruitt's eyes, Strong saw naked terror.

Strong resumed walking and the limb grew gradually narrower. Behind him, Marijane said, "I was thinking of Dandelion this morning."

"It's a pretty planet," Strong said.

"Yes, it is. I—I think this will be far enough."

They turned and faced the camera. There were green leaves and crimson tree flowers above and below and behind and on either side of them. A haha bird winged over their heads. The chinooklike wind came over the plain and caused the leaves to twinkle, mixing the darker greens of their upper surfaces with the lighter greens of their undersides. It was such a lovely scene to have to go to such sad waste.

"Do you have us, Jerry?" Marijane called to Pruitt.

"All set."

"Take, then."

Marijane faced her millions of viewers-to-be. "This is Marijane of Transstar News of the Trans-Astralis Network," she said. "I'm standing here on a limb high in the great big tree on Plains all of you have been watching being cut down, and standing beside me is the heroic man who has been doing the cutting, Mr. Thomas Strong. He has consented to this interview so that all of you can get to know the kind of man it takes to implement such hazardous work." She faced Strong. "Is this the type of work you always do, Mr. Strong?"

Strong, agonizingly aware of the millions of viewers-to-be, managed a simple "Yes." Added to his agony was the agony the woman standing beside him instilled.

"How did you happen to be the tree man selected, Mr. Strong?"

"There are three of us, and when there's a big felling we draw blades of grass," Strong said, feeling like a fool. "The one who draws the longest blade gets to do the actual removal. In this case, I drew it."

"How fascinating." She did not mean to sound cynical, but her voice, perhaps from force of habit, lent the words a sarcastic edge. "Were you pleased to become the one to fell this arboreal monstrosity?"

Strong, cognizant of the idyllic green and crimson scene in which they were being 3Ved, answered, "I don't believe I thought of the tree in words like that. I was afraid of it, but I didn't hate it. To me, it was a job that had to be done. It's the Reapers who hate it."

"And with good cause too." Marijane faced her audience-to-be. "You will see scenes presently of what this tree that our daring Beowulf regards so objectively has done to the lovely houses the Reapers moved into when they came and which they have come to call their own." Back to Strong: "Before you decided to go into tree work, Mr. Strong, what kind of work did you do?"

"I was in school."

"High school?"

"And college."

This surprised her. On Dandelion she had asked him

nothing about his past, nor had he asked anything of hers. He'd already known—or had surmised—the kind of woman she was, and hadn't wanted to think about it. As for her, she knew only that he had grown up somewhere on Earth in the same place Peake had. "I see," she said. "You studied silviculture then, or some similar subject."

"No. You don't need to know anything about trees to cut them down. All you need is a saw. I studied Italian literature."

Marijane was infuriated with herself. She should have sounded out Tom before. Then she would have known which questions to ask and which to eschew. But she'd thought she knew him. And she did too. Knew him insofar as his actions were concerned as well as she knew the Douay Bible her father had given her on her twelfth birthday. Tom had been a gentle bull she led around by the nose—until she inadvertently let the information about Peake slip from her tongue. Then the bull had balked. But she'd never known anything of its past. In God's name, why would anyone who had majored in Italian literature decide to become an ape? And how could she possibly relate Paul Bunyan to Dante, Petrarch, Manzoni, and Moravia?

She would have to play it by ear. "It baffles me, Mr. Strong," she said, "and I'm certain it baffles our viewers too, why a student of Italian literature should suddenly decide to become a tree man—to substitute brachiation for teaching."

"I decided I didn't want to teach," Strong said. He could see the millions of viewers-to-be now, and they terrified him.

"I see." (Thoreau—that was it! She would relate him to Thoreau. No Paul Bunyan, this treeman, but a silent walker of the woods.) "Like Thoreau, you decided that the essence of nature was more in keeping with your thoughts than the brashness of a college campus. You *do* have a sort of quiet, unassuming heroism about you, Mr. Strong."

Catcalls came from Strong's invisible audience. Boos. Its members knew his nakedness. Desperately, he said, "Studying something doesn't mean you have to teach it. I won an athletic scholarship in high school, but I didn't want to take up physical education, so I made arrangements to study a subject that had always interested me."

Marijane pounced on the scholarship. "A scholarship in what field of sport?" she demanded.

"Wrestling."

She remembered the rippling flow of his muscles, the trimness of his waist. Why hadn't she thought to ask? No matter. She now had two relationships to the tree. "A Thoreau who wrestles with the wilderness," she said.

More catcalls. More boos.

"What you are doing here on Plains," Marijane said in her best broadcast Anglo-American, "is a tribute to Man. Man has always fought the eternal forces of nature, first on Earth and then on the umbilical planets. Stood face to face with its droughts, its storms, its floods. Most of all he has fought off the vicious plants that have ever striven to destroy that which he has planted and that which he has built." She faced the camera. "This is Marijane of Trans-Astralis News standing on a big limb high in the last Yggdrasill of Plains."

Except for an occasional call of a haha bird and the small sounds Pruitt made collapsing his camera, it grew silent in the tree. "Well," Marijane said at last, "it was a good interview after all."

Freed from the millions of eyes-to-be that had been upon him, Strong said, "I'm glad it worked out."

"Yes," she said, looking at him. Then she looked up into the sky at the Haus Meiten and waved her arm. Immediately the Haus Meiten began to descend. "Well, it was a long time between times," she said to Strong.

He nodded but said nothing.

The Haus Meiten halted about twenty feet above them and the basket came down. Pruitt stepped into it, carrying the tripodic camera. "Well, thanks, Tom," Marijane said.

"You're welcome."

He watched her walk along the limb and step into the basket. She waved. He waved back. The basket lifted into the Haus Meiten and the craft lifted into the sky. He watched it move off in the direction of the sheds, watched till it disappeared; then he walked back to the trunk of the tree. Still deliberately not thinking, he coiled the end of the rope for a swing and tossed it up and over the stub he'd pulled it down from. The airhauler, he saw, had returned to its previous position. He got back into his saddle and walked back out on the limb. The length of the saddle rope precluded his walking as far out on it as he wanted to, and the first cut he made was sloppy. But it got rid of where Marijane had been.

At five o'clock Bluesky sent the sack back down and lowered Strong's dinner, and water for him to wash, and then the airhauler headed for the sheds. Since the interview Strong had removed four more limbs and again brought the trunk down to base. After removing the limb Marijane had been on he had had to start pegging his saddle rope. It took three cuts now to remove a limb, and the size of the trunk precluded its being cut in sections longer than twenty feet. The middle-sized tongs had barely been able to grasp the final section he'd sent up. Tomorrow they would begin using the big tongs.

Strong washed before he ate, but he didn't bother to shave. He would have a good beard started by the time he finished the tree. Perhaps he would let it go on growing. Although Matthews had said nothing, he sus-

pected that she had again supervised the preparation of
his dinner. It was roast beef this time, and mashed potatoes and gravy, with peas and a tossed salad as vege-
tables. Cold tea in a throwaway vacpac proved to be
the beverage, and there was a large slice of peach pie
for dessert. Most, possibly all, of the food came from
Plains, and it was delicious. Unfortunately he had no
appetite, and ate only a little of this and a little of that
and threw the rest away.

As he sat there on the sack afterward, smoking, Matthews's voice sounded in his left ear. "Dinner okay,
Tom?"

"Sure thing."

"Marijane told me the interview came off fine."

"It seemed to work pretty well."

"You okay up there, Tom? Do you have everything
you need?"

"Sure. Everything."

"You sound so downcast."

"Being downcast is my true nature. There's nothing
to worry about, Matty."

"Fine. I shall stop then. This second. Get a good
night's sleep, Tom. Finis and out."

He sat there on the limb in the last of the day's light,
smoking cigarettes, stubbing them and throwing them
away. He could not see the sunset. The tree's massive
branches and its trillions of leaves hid it from view.
When the last blue blush of the day faded from the sky
he got the tree tent out of the sack and set the tent up
and placed the little campfire before it. But he did not
go inside; instead he sat back down on the sack. The
tree by now was alive with haha birds; the hunters and
the huntresses had returned, and some of them were
seeking out new branches on which to roost. "Why
don't you gang up on me and chase me from the tree?"
Strong asked them. But they went right on hahaing, as
though he wasn't there. Perhaps to them he wasn't, and

even if he was they probably didn't associate his presence with the dwindling of their home.

Gradually the discordant haha chorus toned down to a background of pianissimo chirps that, in turn, toned down to nothing, and now all was silent in the tree. In the sky, the first star came out, and not long afterward Penelope, the first moon, climbed above the far-flung branches of the tree; and still Strong had not moved. Penelope climbed swiftly toward zenith. She was smaller than Earth's sole moon, but far brighter, owing to her terrain. She was ice fields from pole to pole. At length her little sister, Danielle, joined her in the visible sky, and Danielle too was ice fields from pole to pole, and now there were two moons in the sky, and all was silver below, silver and silent and serene.

Beside Strong, Marijane sat. But he would not look at her. He supposed that in one way or another she would always sit beside him. Well, let her, he thought. I won't look at her. I'll never look at her no matter how long she sits there in her obscene nakedness.

The limb on which he sat was an argent pathway bordered by silver leaves. In the bright light of the two moons he could see way out upon it, and the longer he looked, the more like a real pathway it became—a pathway that, were he to follow it, would lead him to the land he'd longed for all his life without ever knowing its true nature, or why he preferred it to the land— the reality—where he had always lived. . . . Sitting there, staring at the faraway leaves at the limb's end, he saw presently that they combined with the double moonlight to form a flower—a pale flower larger and lovelier than any of the others he had found in the tree—and he got up and began walking toward it along the limb.

He walked and walked, and the limb narrowed beneath his feet. Not once did he take his eyes from the flower, and his feet found their own way along the

limb. It began to sway beneath him, but he barely noticed. When he came to the end of it he saw her sitting
on a slender bough and saw that the flower was her
face.

She made room for him on the bough. It bent beneath them. As before, her beauty shocked him. *I'm
glad you're here,* he said. *It was lonely sitting back
there all alone.*

You had someone sitting beside you, she said.

*In a way I did, but how could you possibly have
known that?*

She did not answer the question. Instead she said,
*You didn't want her to sit there, but she sat there any-
way. But even though she would not go away, you were
still alone.*

Yes, he said, *I was still alone.*

And now you're no longer alone.

No. Now I'm with you.

It's dreadful being alone, she said. *I've been alone
for years.*

How old are you? he asked.

I don't know. Not in your years.

Are you as old as the tree?

Yes.

Are you as old as the village?

Oh, I am older than the village. I built the village.

*I don't believe you. You couldn't have built it. Be-
sides, you're too young to be that old.*

There's no need for you to believe me.

*Why did the people who lived in the village kill
themselves?*

Because their tree was dying.

But it wasn't dying.

*Yes. It was dying. They knew when the trees of the
other villages died that theirs was dying too, and for the
same reason. So they didn't wait. They didn't want to
see it die. So when the people who lived in the other*

*villages migrated to the Death Caves and killed them-
selves, the people who lived in this village did too.*

You're implying they worshipped the tree.

*They didn't but their ancestors did, and too late they
realized why.*

*But it wasn't dying. It didn't begin to die till I
climbed down into it and began to kill it.*

No. It has been dying for years.

I don't understand, he said.

You will, she said. *Soon everything will be clear.*

Maybe I can save it. It's not too late.

It was too late long before you climbed into it.

*I don't believe you. If I were to leave it the way it is,
it would live for a thousand years.*

*No. Do you think that if the tree wasn't dying I
wouldn't have beseeched you not to kill it? That I
wouldn't have done everything I could to stop you? But
I knew that you would only be precipitating its death—
that in a way you would be performing an act of mercy.
But I was bitter. That's why, when I first spoke to you
when you were standing in the square, I said,* When I
die, you do too. *I thought I hated you and I wanted to
frighten you. But I didn't hate you. I couldn't. It
wouldn't be you who would be precipitating the tree's
death, it would be the inevitability of which you are a
defenseless part—the same inevitability that had already caused the tree's descent to death.*

The only inevitability I'm a part of, he said, *is the
inevitability of civilization. It has been decided that the
tree must go. Therefore, it will go. If I refused to cut off
another limb, Matthews would send up Peake. And if I
killed Peake I'd have to kill Bluesky, because she would
have to send him up next. And afterward I'd have to go
on killing whoever she or someone else sent up, and
eventually someone would kill me and fell the tree anyway. Is that what you mean by "inevitability"?*

It's part of what I mean.

All right. If it must be done, then, it will be done by my own hand.

So be it, she said.

And if you die when your tree dies, I'll die too. Just as you said.

No.

Yes, he said. *If you die, I don't want to live. I'm in love with you.*

There was a short, silver silence. Then: *You can't possibly be in love with me,* she said.

Why can't I be?

Because—because—

Because in the clear, cold fastnesses of my mind where sanity abides I don't think you're real?

You don't, do you? she said.

I love you whether you're real or not. But I think you're real—even though you don't fit into the little box my reality comes in.

It's true. I'm real. As real as you are, though in a different way.

I know it's true.

You know it now, but will you know it tomorrow?

Yes, he said, and reached out and touched her face. She jerked her head away, but not before he knew the soft coolness of her cheek. The coolness was like the coolness of the double moonlight that reigned around them. Then she grew tenuous in his gaze. *You shouldn't have done that,* she said. *You're trying to make me into something that I'm not—something I don't think I can be. Now we shall have to spend the night alone.*

He felt the bough bend beneath him. He made no effort to reach the limb. He wanted to fall. Down, down through the limbs and leaves to the ground. *Are you going to let your tree kill me?* he asked.

As though in answer, the bough broke, and he began to fall. *This is what I wanted all along,* he thought.

Then he felt her hand seize his wrist and felt himself being lifted to the limb. He heard her voice. *No, never,* she said. He realized then that he had closed his eyes. When he opened them, she was gone.

He walked back the way he had come. Momentarily he expected his acrophobia to descend upon him like a sledgehammer and send him crawling the rest of the way to his tent. But it did not, and suddenly he knew that it wouldn't, couldn't, because it belonged to his other self—the self he had deserted or that had deserted him when it fell silently and invisibly through the understory to the ground.

Matthews sat in the bar beside Bluesky. Peake had retired early. The bar was crowded tonight. The Reapers were celebrating the demise of the tree in advance. Laughter, giggles, shouts, loud music: If you went to one busy bar you had gone to them all. Westermeyer was there with his wife. They stood on Matthews's left. Bluesky stood on her right. The Westermeyers were drinking Magellanic Clouds, Bluesky was drinking straight whiskey. In addition to the Reapers, Marijane and her two cameramen were also present. Marijane kept looking at the door, probably hoping Peake would come in. Let her look, the bitch! Matthews thought. And then she thought, Sugar and Spice and Everything Vice. She sipped the Old Earth she had ordered.

Westermeyer's wife was telling Matthews about the new rotted-out area she had found in her house. It wasn't as bad as the first one, but it was bad enough. It was in the living room, under one of the windows. "We arranged the curtains so it wouldn't show," she said. On Matthews's other side Bluesky was talking to Katerina, who was tending bar, about "the little people." Matthews found Bluesky's conversation more interesting than Westermeyer's wife's. She had been listening to women like Westermeyer's wife all her life. "Lordy,"

Westermeyer's wife said, "we'll be glad to get that dirty tree out of here!"

On Matthews's right, Bluesky said, "When the little people came, the big people would turn out all the lights and sit around and stomp their feet."

"The big people being your ancestors," Katerina said.

"Right. They'd sit there in the dark room and stomp their feet so loud they couldn't hear the little people any more than they could see them. That way, nobody could say the little people didn't come. I tell you, I had clever ancestors."

"That's no way to talk about one of the noblest cultures in American history."

"They were a bunch of old women," Bluesky said. "They thought rocks and mountains and trees were supernatural beings."

"Animism."

"Right. Animism."

Katerina had to go down the bar and wait on one of the other customers. She was wearing a short orange dress that left all of her back except her buttocks bare. When she came back she said, "Animism's common among primitive cultures. Take the Quantextil, for example."

"Because they worshipped the tree? Yes, I guess it adds up to that. They were a bunch of old women too."

Katerina again had to leave to wait on someone. On Matthews's left, Westermeyer said across his wife's big breasts, "We ought to throw this boy of yours up in the tree a party when he gets done."

"Tom wouldn't like that," Matthews said. "He's not the party type."

"Sure he'd like it. He may pretend not to like being a hero, but underneath he's like everybody else. And the Reapers will love the idea. You don't realize how we feel about that tree, Ms. Matthews. It's like a plague that attacks houses instead of people, and when you have houses like ours it's almost as though the plague attacked you."

"Well, if you want to, go ahead. But I still don't think he'll like it."

"Good. I'll get the ball rolling tomorrow. We'll hold it here in the hotel. It'll have the added beneficence of giving us something to do. You've probably noticed that for us this is a slack time of year. When the wheat's ready we'll work like tornadoes. And we'll work like tornadoes seeding the second crop. But right now, except for reconnaissance, there's next to nothing to do."

"If you planted winter wheat you could get three crops a year."

"Squeezing out two crops during spring, summer, and fall doesn't leave enough time. In winter, we plant Plains alfalfa and strip-plow it under early in spring. It works out quite well that way."

"You've got gold dust in your soil."

Westermeyer grinned. "At least the equivalent of it."

On Matthews's right Bluesky said, "Another whiskey, Kate."

When she brought it, he said, "The reason I make fun of my own people is that they were so dumb. If there'd been enough of them and they'd had the know-how, they'd have done the same things the white man did."

"But they didn't, did they?" Matthews interposed.

"No, Matty, they didn't, and that's what makes the story. That's what lifts the curtain on the buffalo."

"Why the buffalo?" Katerina asked. "You told me you were a Seneca. There weren't any buffalo in your backyard."

"Right. All there was was corn. The saddest corn you ever saw—about as long as a stringbean and not a hell of a lot thicker. You can't go to war about corn like that. But with the buffalo it was different. The buffalo were there. Nobody grew them. They were. And then the white man came and almost destroyed them. They may not have been in my backyard, but they were in the Indians' backyard, and I'm an Indian. Fifty million of them, there were. Fifty million! And when the white man got done there were only five hundred!"

"I think he's drunk," Westermeyer whispered across his wife's breasts.

"Singing," Matthews said. She finished her Old Earth. "Well, you people, I think it's time I went to bed."

"But don't you think *he* should go to bed?" Westermeyer whispered again. "I mean, you've got a man up there in the tree and the Indian's going to be running the winch tomorrow, and—"

"And he'll run it as efficiently as he always does," Matthews said. "Good night, everybody. Finis and out."

V

Yggdrasill astralis

Bark: Varies in color from black in the understory to dark gray in the overstory. In the
understory, particularly on the trunk and those
areas of the limbs nearest it, the epidermis is
characterized by prominences alternating with
fissures, some of the latter of which, near the
tree's base, reach depths of 5'–6'.

BLUESKY arose before dawn. He always arose before
dawn no matter where he was or how much he had
drunk the night before. This morning he was in Katerina's bedroom, and he had drunk a lot the night before.
But he felt no different from having drunk a lot than he
would have felt had he drunk only a little. When he
wasn't drinking he lived in an interface of drunkenness
and sobriety.

Katerina still slept soundly. He did not awaken her.
Instead he dressed silently in the pink radiance coming
through the window. The room's own light was covered
with a black shield. It was a charming room. When he
had first seen it last night in its own light, Bluesky had
thought it was a child's room. But the size of the bed
gave lie to that. The room had only one flaw. The ceiling above the bed was beginning to rot away.

He left the room and walked through the living room
to the front door and let himself out into the dawn. He

became instantly aware of the tree. Katerina's house was quite close to the square, and from where he stood he could not see where the tree's overstory had been, and it was as if the tree had not been cut at all, as if it were still as tall and intact as it had been before removal had begun.

As he walked down the street toward the square, Katerina vanished from the small section of his mind he had briefly set aside for her. He was south of the tree, and the dawnlight lay upon his right cheek and temple as he walked. The tree grew as he neared it, presently became the sky. He could hear the arising haha birds hahaing up among the leaves and the branches. He thought of Strong up there among them, and he was glad it was Strong and not himself. He hadn't wanted the tree. Not because he had feared it, but because he was sick of killing trees. Sick of this ultimate evidence of his whitemanization.

The square, with its grotesque birdbath, as yet showed no evidence of the cutting. Tomorrow it would. Tomorrow there would be great limbs lying in it; great trunk sections, and he and Peake would descend from their mechanical aerie and begin making the splits that would have to be made before the limbs and the sections could be lifted and carried away. But now the square was clean in the brightening dawnlight, the bark-clad pillar of the tree lifting magnificently up into the green and black sky of its leaves and limbs, of which it was the sole support.

The hotel stood five blocks from the street he had just left. He set off toward it in long yet leisurely strides. He was in no hurry to get there. Dawn was his favorite time of day. During dawn he thought of the past of his people. The past he made fun of when he was wholly drunk and tried to let on that he didn't take seriously. The past was where he wanted to be. Not the semicivilized past where people sat in dark rooms and stomped their feet waiting for the little people, but the remote past. Way back in the thick forests of Stone Age North America. Perhaps he would not belong there, but he did not belong here either. Perhaps he belonged nowhere.

Beneath the tree dawn's breath held a hint of green. He walked in the green pinkness, thinking of Deganawida. "Two water currents flowing together." Deganawida, like Christ, had been born of a virgin. He was a Huron. When he grew up he set forth in his silver-birch canoe to form the Five Nations. Bluesky saw him on the river in his White Canoe. He saw the melting ice along the river's edges and knew the time was spring. Bluesky envied him, yearned for the savage land through which the Huron would pass. The old place names—Protruding Rocks, On the Hillside, I have Daubed It, Broken Branches Lying, Old Clearing— passed through his mind. He saw the places in the green pinkness beneath the tree, but he saw them with his own eyes, not Deganawida's. The jaundiced eyes of an Indian out of step with time.

And yet not altogether out of step. The Indians used to kill trees. When their wretched corn wouldn't grow they killed trees and made new gardens, because the soil where the trees stood was always fertile. And it would remain fertile for a while, and then more trees would have to be killed for new gardens. But there were so many trees then it hadn't mattered. Even after the white man came and began killing them it hadn't mattered—not at first. But the white man had gone wild. At first he killed trees mainly to plant his own gardens and to build cabins to live in, but after a while he began killing them for every reason under the sun. He hadn't killed quite all of them, but he would have, so he would have paper to write on and paper with which to wipe his lips and his ass, and room for roads and parking lots and buildings. Yes, he'd have killed all of them if the trans-astralis drive hadn't been developed, killed every tree on Earth eventually, all the while pretending he wasn't. But the trans-astralis drive had saved what forests still remained, and now tree killing was relegated to other worlds, and here I am, Bluesky thought, helping to kill them, not for a garden where I can grow corn, but for all sorts of reasons. Take this crazy tree—what am I helping to kill it for? To keep houses from rotting away. Well, anyway, that's a slightly different reason. At least I'm not helping to kill it so people can read dirty books.

His "journey" through Protruding Rocks, On the Hillside, I have Daubed It, Broken Branches Lying, and Old Clearing had brought him to the hotel. He climbed the two flights of stairs to the third floor and knocked on Matthews's door. Her voice when she answered seemed to come from far away. "It's Owen, Matty," he answered. "You wanted somebody to wake you up."

After a long while she said, "Thanks, Owen," and he went down to the dining hall for breakfast.

In the tree, Strong breakfasted again on cheeseggs and ham and coffee. He smoked a cigarette on the morning limb, then he struck the tree tent and returned it and the campfire to the sack. He lowered the sack to a limb far below him. Then he began walking out on the limb on which he stood. Acrophobia did not touch him. He did not stop walking till the limb began bending beneath him. He was far enough out on it by then to see the bough. It was broken and its leaves had already begun to pale. He was not surprised. He had known it would be there and that it would be broken. But he had wanted to see it, to underline it with the light of day to emphasize a fantasy that had become fact.

If it must be done, then it will be done by my own hand.

Yes.

He walked part of the way back to the trunk and sat down to await the airhauler.

But it'll be all right, he told himself. I know she said that when a dryad's tree dies she dies too, and I know she doesn't lie. But she doesn't know that this is true. She only thinks it is. So when her tree dies I'll take her with me, I'll see to it that she doesn't die, I won't let her. "I won't let her," he said aloud.

Genji the sun hadn't lifted high enough to bathe the stubbed top of the tree, and the light in which Strong sat seemed green from the ambient leaves. He liked the light that way. He even liked the calls of the haha birds that came from below. Living in the tree, he had begun to like the tree. But he couldn't permit this, of course, so when such thoughts preceded the appearance of the airhauler, he shoved them to one side and thought of the dryad. But that was almost as bad, because the tree was her home.

When Bluesky sent down the big tongs Strong aligned their great teeth with the sides of the limb, and Bluesky raised the cable and the teeth bit into the bark and the bast. Strong went back toward the trunk and made the first cut, and the workday began.

He got rid of the limb in three sections. Big ones. Soon he would have to go to four. The Haus Meiten came into the sky. He ignored it. Flights of haha birds were spreading out over the plain. While he was waiting on the next limb Matthews said, "Good morning, everyone," and he and Peake and Bluesky returned the greeting. "Be careful up there, Tom," she said. "You're in the big woods now."

"I will be," Strong said.

"Finis and out."

She laid the transmitter back down on the table. She was all alone in the dining hall. All alone with the dream from which Bluesky had awakened her. She had wanted someone to awaken her because she had been awakening at four in the morning and reliving all the bad parts of her life till dawn, and then sinking into a deep sleep that returned the second she shut off the alarm. But last night it had been different, last night she hadn't awakened at four, she had gone right on sleeping, and she had dreamed she was the tree.

At first she hadn't known she was the tree. She had known only that she was standing all alone in what appeared to be a vast, dark-gold field. But she could see simultaneously in all directions—quite how she did not know, for she had no eyes—and presently in the dim dawnlight in which she stood she discerned the tiny blocks that encircled her just within the beginning of the dark-gold field, and realized they were houses and that she was the tree.

But she wasn't the tree as it was now. She was the tree as it had been before Tom had descended into its branches with his terrible saw. Tall and proud, yet strangely sad, commanding the dark-gold plain.

As she stood there in the dim dawnlight awaiting the arrival of her friend the sun, she became aware of her multitudinous limbs and her countless leaves. She felt nutrient-carrying water welling up through her xylem and she felt the chloroplasts of her leaves processing the first light of the new day. She knew the breeze that began to breathe across the plain. She knew her transpiration. She rejoiced in the infinitesimal creatures that lived in her green breast, that foraged far and wide over the plain; that built nests each spring and copulated among her leaves. She knew the meiofauna in the soil beneath her that recycled the wastes into matter that helped to give her life.

The sun rose and day came, and now she knew the

vivid Van Gogh sky above her verdant head and the
breeze that had become a wind. She knew the crimson
flowers of her green bodice. Time picked up a pace. A
thousand paces. Dusk came, then night, then day again.
A flickering succession of brightnesses and darknesses.
Summer appeared with its rich warmth, and sometimes
storms formed far out on the plain and walked on black
legs across the land. Summer, then fall, and now the
countless sterile nuts she had grown began to drop, and
after them, her leaves. She slept naked but warm
through the cold winds and the snows that followed,
and when she awakened, it was spring. But now she
knew a hunger she had been unaware of before. Yet it
had been there, she knew, for a long time, intensifying
with each day till finally it touched her being, informing
her that something was wrong. She searched her envi-
rons for the wrongness, and at last she unearthed it.
When she saw what it was, she cried. She was still
crying in her sleep when Bluesky knocked. "Yes?" she
answered. And then "Thanks, Owen," she said. She lay
there in the dawnlight, trying to remember what the
wrongness was. But she couldn't.

Nor could she now, sitting in the dining hall over her
second cup of coffee. All she could think of was how
beautiful she had been standing there tall and proud on
the dark-gold plain. It occurred to her after a while that
her hollowness was gone. Sadness filled her now, and a
sense of wonder about the tree.

Strong made good progress despite the difficulty the
girth of the limbs and the trunk now presented. Each
limb had to be removed in four sections, and he had to
split the trunk lengths before cutting them horizontally,
otherwise the tongs would not have been able to grip
them. But when noon came he was deep in the understory.

Bluesky sent down his lunch. Strong ate half of one

of the sandwiches and threw the rest of the food away, except the coffee. He drank the coffee, smoking cigarettes. He had already lowered the sack twice. Now he had to lower it again. It knocked off tree-flower petals on the way down, but they no longer disturbed him. He had become used to the sight of the tree's "blood." Moreover, he was a machine now, a machine self-programmed to destroy the home of the woman he loved. When the sack was in place he withdrew the rope and attacked the tree again.

The haha birds that hadn't departed for the plain were screaming their raucous laughter now and making wild flights from limb to limb. They knew now that their abode was in jeopardy. They no longer left the limb sections Strong cut till the section was airborne, and then they winged frantically back into the tree. At length, beneath a burst of foliage, Strong came to a man-made wooden building that circled the massive trunk. He stared at it. It was a birdhouse.

His consternation derived less from the presence of the house than from how it had gotten there. It was well built, but in places it had all but rotted away, and in those places where it hadn't at least a foot of droppings covered the floor. The droppings were old, and the lack of any recent droppings indicated the house had not been in use for a long time. The walls that hadn't rotted away were perforated at precise intervals with holes large enough for a haha bird to get through, and inside the walls remnants of a few perches remained. Clearly he was regarding a Quantextil artifact—one that could have been in the tree for as long as a century. But how had the Quantextil lifted it up there? Or, as was probably the case, if they had built it in the tree how had they lifted the necessary material?

With ropes, of course. But that brought him down to the basic question: How had *they* gotten up there?

The answer was the same. With ropes.

According to AnthropoCo they had lived on wheat alone, but AnthropoCo wasn't God, and it was conceivable that they had abetted their diet with small game. Such an assumption demanded a weapon for them to have hunted the game with, and the most logical weapon would have been a bow and arrows. A strong hunter with a strong enough bow could have got a light line over the tree's lowest limb, after which a rope could have been drawn over it. Then one of the Quantextil could have made the awesome climb and, at the end of it, have clambered to the top of the limb by means of the prominences and fissures. Or they could have rigged a block and tackle and pulled him up. That was probably how they had worked it. Then they had sent up another rope, and the Quantextil in the tree had used it somehow to gain the limb Strong stood on now and to transfer the block and tackle and the main rope.

A simple enough procedure. Nevertheless, it dissatisfied Strong. It was based on too many assumptions. But for the moment it was the only answer he could come up with.

A second examination of the birdhouse suggested that much of it must have been built on the ground and then lifted into place. It was too ornate to have been built entirely in the tree. Picturing it as it must have looked in its long-ago heyday, he found that it had been ugly. There was too much unnecessary molding. There were even little cupolas on the sections of the roof that hadn't rotted. He added them to the picture in his mind. He came up with a gingerbread house.

Despite its size it couldn't even have begun to accomodate all the birds that lived in the tree. Maybe when it had been built there hadn't been so many birds. Or maybe—and he knew suddenly that this was the true answer—most of the birds that now lived in the tree were the descendants of birds that had lived in the

other trees and that had migrated when those trees had
died.

But why in the worlds had the Quantextil gone to
such fantastic lengths to build the gingerbread house?

He recalled the big birdbath in the square and the
much smaller birdbaths that still remained in their converted states in most of the backyards of Bigtree. No
question about it, the Quantextil had loved the birds.
But love alone couldn't account for the birdhouse in the
tree. They must have worshipped the birds.

Why?

Strong could find no answer.

A voice sounded in his left ear. Bluesky's. "Tom, you
there?"

Strong tongued on his transmitter. "Sure I'm here."

"Thought maybe you'd gone for a beer."

Man became machine again, and the stream of lofted
limb and trunk sections resumed its flow. Strong could
not wholly free his thoughts from the birdhouse,
though, not even when the last two cuts of the day removed it from his milieu. The sight of it created mild
consternation up above and in the hotel dining room.
"You been building a treehouse, Tom?" Peake wanted
to know.

"Tom, what is that damn thing?" Matthews asked.

"It's a birdhouse," Strong said.

"So it is," said Bluesky.

"Christ!" Peake said. "Those dumb Druids had it
with the birds too!"

Since finding the birdhouse, or perhaps since thinking about it, Strong had discovered that the sides of the
prominences were extremely rough and provided hand-
and footholds, and that in many places, by remaining in
one of the fissures, he could climb up and down the
trunk. Was this how the birdhouse builders had climbed
around in the tree? He knew suddenly that it was, and
knew that this was probably how they had climbed up

the lower trunk. They could have brought their rope
with them. The depths of the fissures in the lower trunk
virtually guaranteed a safe route into the tree.

The Haus Meiten had vanished from the sky in midafternoon. Marijane probably had a hundred times
more footage of him than she could use. Now the airhauler returned from delivering the final limb to the
huge pile in the processing yard, and Bluesky lowered
water for him to wash and his dinner. Corned beef and
cabbage. Iced tea to drink. Ice cream and apple pie for
dessert. He ate mechanically, barely tasting the food.
When he finished he decided to climb the way the
Quantextil had, and he pulled his saddle rope through
the last peg he'd driven, coiled it and looped it over his
shoulder. Then he began the short descent to the sack,
moving between two of the great bark prominences. It
worked well. Yes, this must have been how the birdhouse builders had got up the trunk. Perhaps other
Quantextil had climbed the tree too. It dawned on him
presently that he was thinking about the Quantextil so
he wouldn't think of the dryad, because the long day
had undermined his conviction that she was real. Simultaneously he came to a huge limb beyond which the
fissure he was descending extended deep into the tree.
Deeper than he could reach. Exploring farther, he
found that the walls of the prominences that formed the
fissure did not come all the way together and that there
was a narrow passage through which he could move.
Entering it, he felt a floor beneath his feet.

In her room at the hotel, Marijane sat in the shielded
light watching the unedited footage of what she had
come to think of not as the tape of the tree but as the
tape of Tom. Occasionally telescopic close-ups of his
face that Jerry had caught filled the entire screen, and
she could see how silklike his thinning hair was and
how dreamlike his light hazel eyes were. His beard, as

the tape progressed, grew gradually longer, and it had the same silklike aspect as his hair. Here was not the Thoreau she had tried to turn him into during the interview. Here, instead, was a poor poet without poetry—a shy, sensitive man who once had loved her. Here was the paraclete the Christ whose values she had trampled had sent to redeem her.

Had she known it then?

Scene: A crowded dance floor in a Dandelion city. *Dramatis personae:* A long-legged, black-haired girl and a man with thinning hair dancing together.

HE: I'm Tom. Thomas Strong.

SHE: We don't need to know each other's names.

HE: I know. But I'd like to know yours.

SHE: Marijane.

HE: Marijane what?

SHE: Just Marijane. It used to be Mary Janus. I shortened it.

HE: I'll bet you're not from Dandelion.

SHE: No. I was born on Mother.

HE: So was I. I know it's none of my business, but what're you doing here?

SHE: I'm taking holographs. I'm a network holographer.

HE: Holographs of who?

SHE: Not who. What. The Grand Abyss. The Teelinguit Cascade. The Vale of Waterfalls. The Stippled Mountains. I'm doing a travelogue for fill-ins.

HE: I'm here to remove trees.

SHE: Good for you.

HE: It's nice meeting someone like you, Marijane. You—you don't know what it means to me to meet someone like you.

SHE: Sure I do. I'm the girl weary wanderers always meet when they're dying on the desert.

HE: I didn't mean it that way.

SHE: How did you mean it?

HE: I was trying to say that, that—I was trying to say that I needed to meet someone like you.

SHE: That's what I said you said.

HE: I—I mean I'd like us to go out together some time.

SHE: Who knows? Maybe some time we will.

HE: I'm serious, Marijane.

SHE: Don't be—it'll get you nowhere.

HE: Please don't be cynical, Marijane.

SHE: Christ! You don't even know how to ask, do you?

No, she had not known it then.

She was glad the day was almost over. She had quit early so she could review the tapes. The day had started out badly. It had begun with the residue of last night's Magellanic Clouds dulling the brightness of the morning, and with the fingers of the dream, which had replayed itself during the night and shocked her awake, still imbedded in her brain. Angry when Peake hadn't showed up in the bar, she had slept alone, telling Jerry, who had reassumed his role as protector, to get lost and ignoring the invitation in Johnny-Boy Dastard's eyes.

Not much could have come from a day with so malevolent a beginning, and not much had. Trouble with the Tri-Henderson recorder, trouble with the X-Hood feeder, trouble with this, trouble with that. The day's tapes were on the screen now, and they were wretched. But there were a few good shots she could use. One of Tom affixing a tree peg and then walking out on a limb as large as a bridge. One of an outer limb section breaking away from the tree and its tiny red flower petals raining down on the village as the airhauler carried it away. She began to feel better, sitting there watching; and then the damned dream came back, and there she was, back in her mind, crushing the meadow flowers, then climbing the horrid "hill." The screen before her held a close-up of her paraclete's face. He seemed to be watching her. She deactuated the screen and ran to the window and opened it and looked out. She could see the roofs of houses, and backyards, and children playing in sandboxes. The house nearest the hotel had a ragged hole in its smooth, shingleless roof. It's rotting away like me, she thought. The whole village is rotting away. The whole world is rotting away. All the worlds, and all the stars and all the island universes. Rotting, rotting away. . . .

The rotted area in the back wall of Westermeyer's house had expanded, and now the exquisite steps that climbed to the back porch and the rear door of the house were afflicted. The outer door now hung on only one wooden hinge. He stood half in the shadow of the house next door and half in the long afternoon rays of Genji the sun staring helplessly at the dead wood. His wife, who had called the new inroads to his attention the minute he got home, stood beside him. "I just noticed it this afternoon," she said.

"Why our house?" Westermeyer demanded. "Why not the others too?"

"It's not just our house—you know that. Lots of the other houses are rotting too."

Westermeyer pressed his finger against part of the rotted area. His finger sank into it all the way up to the second knuckle. He felt sick.

Although his increasing paranoia indicated otherwise, he knew better than his wife that theirs was not the only house afflicted. He himself had been the instrument that had effected the Reapers' decision to remove the tree. When the first evidence of decay appeared in one of the outlying houses and was brought to his attention, a single heinous word had exploded in his mind: *Blight!* BotaniCo maintained a small lab in Helisport, and he had taken a sample of the rotted wood there at once. Since the blight that had destroyed the other villages and the other trees was hypothetical, the BotaniCo specialists had had nothing specific to look for, but this had not proved to matter. The minute life-forms they found in the wood (they said) were a Plains species of saprophytic fungi—the type of fungi that attacks wood that is already dead. One of the specialists accompanied Westermeyer to Bigtree, and after looking at the decayed area firsthand had made the pronouncement that doomed the tree: "Excessive transpiration and excessive shade—they're your enemies, Doctor Westermeyer. They're what's rotting your houses." (By then several more houses had been afflicted.) Westermeyer had said nothing about removing the tree, but only because he hadn't needed to. The Reapers had wanted it removed ever since they'd experienced its leaf fall during their first autumn on Plains. All Westermeyer had needed to do was pick up the torch. He had done so.

He probed again with his finger. It sank into the rotting wood even deeper than before.

He turned and faced the tree. From where he stood it seemed as tall and as stalwart as it had three days ago. Its insouciance incensed him. He had never liked trees. He had been born near the Great North American Desert where there were very few trees, and prior to his inclusion in the Bigtree Co-operative he had been teaching an advanced course in agriculture in an open-air educational institution in a Mexican reclamation area where there were no trees at all. The Bigtree tree had frightened him at first; it had frightened all the Reapers. Just looking at it had been enough for him to want it removed. Maybe the tree had known that. Maybe that was why it had attacked his house and not the ones next door. Maybe the tree knew him as well as, perhaps better than, he knew himself. Maybe it had

thought, Look at this poor creature who thinks he was
born to conduct the task to which he has been assigned,
who thinks he has finally found his Lebensraum. Who
thinks to find in wheat all those subtle intangibles that
all his life have eluded him. Who in his mind sees gold
growing on the plain that surrounds me and who will do
all he can to keep that gold to himself and to his immediate compeers. Who sees the village as his own. Who
hated me before I lifted a finger against him. Look at
this wretched being from another world who in his
mind presumes my destruction!

Westermeyer braked the train of his thoughts before
its sick wheels could roll any farther. He had stopped at
the hotel on his way home and had looked at Matthews's screens, and he knew that however tall the tree
might seem to stand, it was a travesty of its former self
and that by tomorrow night it would be gone. Or, if not
gone, a pile of dying wood in the square or in the processing mill yard. Yggdrasill, like Ozymandias, fallen.
Then let's see you rot my house! he thought. Then let's
see you contemn my birthright! I own the village, tree!
I own the wheat! Tomorrow night I'll own the ground
you stand on!

The floor Strong stood on was smooth. The fissure
turned right, then left. But little daylight remained in
the tree, and now none of it reached him. Suddenly the
walls of the fissure ceased to be. He stopped then and
got his cigarette lighter from his pocket. He flicked it
on. He found himself standing just within the narrow
doorway of a grotto.

Directly before him a narrow aisle divided two rows
of wooden benches. It led to a large object that stood
against the opposite wall. The flickering light thrown by
his lighter refused to reveal what the object was, and he
walked toward it down the aisle. He stopped several
feet in front of it and stared.

It was a tree.

It was *this* tree. Brought down to size so that it was but little larger than he.

Above it hung a hammock that had been woven of leaves.

The light of the lighter had steadied, but it told him no more than he knew already. Surely the grotto must contain some source of light. A darker area on the wall to his right caught his eye, and approaching it, he found it was a small niche and that there was a candle in it. A film of dust covered the candle's wick, and he flicked the dust away and brought the candle to life.

There was a similar niche and candle on the opposite wall, he saw. Crossing the grotto, he lit that candle too, then extinguished his lighter and returned it to his pocket. His saddle rope was still hanging from his shoulder. He removed the rope and laid it on the nearest bench. He could see the room quite clearly now. It was roughly square, about twenty by twenty feet. The ceiling was about ten feet high. The floor was polished. A film of dust covered it, but he could see the tree's rings through the dust. He could see them on the ceiling too. The walls were also polished, and there were pictures on them. Paintings. The benches that covered most of the floor were also filmed with dust. There were tree rings on them too. When the room was carved, they had been carved also. They were extensions of the floor. Like most of the furniture in the houses of the village. But they lacked the furniture's grace.

Carved? Who could possibly have carved a grotto this size out of the tree? Who but the Quantextil? But why?

He looked at the model tree. They had carved that too.

He returned to it in the candlelight and stood before it. It was so realistic that standing there was like standing before the real tree. He felt big. Huge. He looked at the thousands of carved arabesques, and the curves and the indentations, that represented the foliage. Once, probably, it had been painted leaf green. The dust on the floor around the tree was much thicker than the dust elsewhere. Probably it comprised flakes of paint. But the foliage now was the same color as the trunk. The trunk and the benches and the floor and the ceiling. And the walls too, except where the paintings were. Probably at one time the trunk had been painted also. Black. But it wasn't now. Like the foliage and most of the room, it was half gold, half brown. But other than for its unrealistic color, the model tree was almost a dead image for the real tree. Not the real tree as it was now, but as it had been before Strong descended into its branches with his beamsaw.

He raised his eyes to the hammock. It hung from the ceiling on metallic cords. The leaves with which it was woven were imitation leaves, and their green coloring was part of them. But they too were filmed with dust. He seized the hammock and shook it. He jerked on the cords to see if they were worn. They did not break. He continued shaking the hammock till the last of the dust fell free and the leaves looked back at him like the real leaves of the tree. He released it then and stood there staring at it.

"Well," he said after a long time, "I've found your home."

But she did not live there anymore—if, indeed, she ever really had.

He next examined the paintings on the walls. They made him think of the paintings, detailed photographs of which he had once seen, on the walls of the cavern of *Les Trois Frères*. He proceeded clockwise around the grotto. Before time had dimmed the paint the artist or artists had used, the paintings must have possessed a Van Gogh vividness, for the colors were distinct even now. One painting depicted three haha birds on the wing. Another, a human figure—probably that of a Quantextil—wielding a scythe. A third, the tree leafed out in summer. The fourth, and last, a girl sitting on a slender bough.

Strong knelt and leaned closer to the picture of the girl, for he knew who she was. Despite the dearth of detail, there was no mistaking those long and graceful legs, those delicate arms, that burst of sun-bright hair, those bright blue eyes. She sat there on the bough exactly the way he had seen her last night, her feet buried in a burst of leaves, her delicate fingers gripping the bough, her blue eyes gazing straight ahead. At him.

He sat down on the floor at her feet. He could not move. He no longer wanted to. I knew last night when I touched you, you were real, he thought. I knew again this morning when I looked at the bough that broke. But if I hadn't known before, I would know now.

And he knew too that she knew he was there, and that if he waited, she would come.

Bluesky went to the bar early. He was Katerina's first customer. When she brought him his whiskey, he saw that she was crying. "Hey," he said, "you don't cry on that side of the bar. It's this side you cry on."

She touched the tears away with the edge of her apron. "My house is rotting away."

"Sure, I saw this morning. But you can get it fixed."

She pointed toward the farther wall. "The hotel's starting to go too. The whole village."

He looked at where she pointed, saw a large darkened area. "Well," he said, "that's why we're removing the tree—right?"

"You think it'll stop when the tree's gone?"

"That's what Westermeyer says."

"I don't know what we'll do if it doesn't."

"Hell," Bluesky said, "you people didn't come here

to live in pretty houses. You came here to get rich fast so you could go back to Earth and live in supercondominiums and slog around in swimming pools all day."

"Maybe that's the way it was before we moved into the houses. Now we don't want to leave. We want to stay. The houses did something to us."

A Reaper came in and stood at the bar several feet from Bluesky. He was in his late twenties and he had a long, sad face. Katerina went to wait on him. When he got his drink he looked at Bluesky. "Thank God you treemen came," he said. "My house is rotting away."

"We're always there in the wings waiting to save people," Bluesky said. "Another whiskey, Kate."

Gradually the bar filled. Marijane came in with Dastard and Pruitt. Pruitt hovered just behind her, even after she sat down on one of the bar stools. Westermeyer and his wife. Westermeyer looked ill. Other Reapers. Matthews showed up, still wearing her plaid shirt, breeches, and boots. At length Peake showed. He stood beside Bluesky. When he caught Katerina's eye, he held up his hand with his forefinger an eighth of an inch from his thumb to show how much Scotch he wanted in his soda.

"Going to watch us clowns do our act again?" Bluesky asked.

"Best show around," Peake said.

Bluesky drank his whiskey, caught Katerina's eye for another. "Poor old Tom up in the tree," he said.

"He belongs up there." Peake looked down the bar at Marijane. She looked back.

"Same show as the other night," Bluesky said.

"Sure," Peake said. He picked up his glass and started down the bar. "See you tomorrow, Injun."

Strong must have dozed off. When he opened his eyes he was still alone in the grotto.

He became aware of how tired he was. Three days now in the tree. He felt that if he tried he wouldn't be able to lift his arms or move his legs. There was fuzz around the edges of his vision.

He leaned back against the wall and presently he dozed off again. When next he opened his eyes he saw that she had come. She was standing just within the fissure, candlelight dancing on her legs, her tunic, her face. There was a tree flower tucked in her hair.

She came over to where he was sitting and sat down beside him. *I didn't know whether to come,* she said. *And then I thought, we can't spend our last night alone.*

Is this your home? he asked.

No. It used to be my temple. The early Quantextil built it for me. The later Quantextil never came near the tree and they never saw me. She pointed to the hammock. *When the early Quantextil climbed up here to worship, they pretended I was in the hammock, sleeping in the tree.*

He said, *Was it you they worshipped, or was it the tree?*

They worshipped both of us, she said.

And the birds too?

Oh, yes. They worshipped the birds. The birds were vital to their way of life.

I don't understand.

I think you do, she said. *Underneath, where you hide your truths.*

He could smell her fragrance. It was green and sweet, like the tree's. He said, *Last night, when the bough broke and I fell, you pulled me back to the limb. Why didn't you let me fall?*

I didn't want anyone else to kill the tree.

I—I thought . . .

What was it you thought? That I saved you because I love you?

Yes. I thought that. But I can see now it couldn't be

true. How could a dryad love the monster who's tearing down her home?

I do love you in a way.

I'm glad of that. I don't think I could go on if you didn't.

You have to go on. You're part of the inevitability.

I still don't fully understand what you mean.

I mean a stage of civilization—a plateau your race climbed upon long ago.

I'm afraid I can't relate that to an inevitability.

But you can. All races climb upon it sooner or later.

What happened to the other trees?

The same thing that happened to this one at a later date. Their worshippers climbed upon the plateau. They became sophisticated. And the more sophisticated they became, the more they ridiculed the customs of their forebears. At length they called those customs superstitious and abrogated them. They discovered new and complex ways of accomplishing simple tasks. What offended them most was the way their forebears had buried their dead. And what offended them almost as much were their forebears' primitive sewage disposal methods. So they abandoned the burial mounds underneath the tree and built a crematory for their dead, and then they built a disposal system that virtually annihilated their wastes. Blinded by their technological sophistication, they refused any longer to pay respect either to the tree or the birds that lived in its branches.

I don't understand, he said.

You will. Tomorrow you'll understand.

*I wish—*he began.

What is it that you wish?

I wish that this was Earth and you and I were lovers walking in the rain and that we'd come to a cottage waiting by the roadside, waiting there for us, and that we would go inside. I wish that we could make love.

Even though I'm real, she said, *I'm not real in the same sense you are.*

I don't care, he said. *I still want to make love to you. Why?*

Because I love you, and making love to you is the only way I can truly express the way I feel.

All men kill the thing they love, she said.

You stole that from my mind too, didn't you?

Yes, I stole it. It was there, hiding among the green thoughts. . . . I have certain powers. I can see into minds. I can make people dream. I can change people in little ways. I can make them look at their own souls. But great changes are beyond me.

Wilde was right. Men do kill the things they love. But what he said isn't true in the present instance.

It may be true without your knowing it.

No, he said, *it isn't true.* And then he said, *I'm tired.*

I know. You're tired, and you want to sleep. And you want to sleep with me.

Do you think it's possible, he said, *for two different phases of reality to become one for a little while?*

It's possible, she said, *but there are no guarantees. Please sleep with me.*

In the bed the Quantextil built for me?

Yes. In your bed.

She rose to her feet and, using the indentations made by the foliage of the model tree, climbed up into the hammock. He climbed up and lay down beside her. *And we are here as on a darkling plain,* she said, and he said, *You stole that from my mind,* and she answered, *Yes,* and the artificial leaves of which their couch was woven became real leaves, and they lay together side by side high in the branches of the tree, and he whispered into her ear, *Will it be all right?* and she answered, *Yes,* and the tree swayed gently beneath them and her flesh was cool and soft, there among the green leaves and the fragrant tree flowers, cool and soft and sweet and timeless, and he said, *Do you love me too?* and she answered, *Yes,* and the leaves rustled beneath them in the night and the stars looked down and the moons paused in their voyages across the sky as time ceased to be and reality folded in upon itself and that which could never be was.

"We shouldn't even be here," Peake said. "Why couldn't we have gone to your room?"

"I like it here beneath the tree," Marijane said.

"Nature girl."

"If you like. But if we'd gone to my room we'd of had Jerry to contend with. He thinks it's partly his."

"We could of gone to mine."

"No. It's better here."

He laughed. She was standing with her back to the tree, and she could see his body vaguely outlined against the lights of the nearer houses. She felt his hand on her hip in the darkness, felt it slide down to her thigh. His other hand lay upon the small of her back, and now he pulled her away from the tree. "I don't like the tree," he said.

"Forget the tree," she whispered.

"I'll try."

They lay upon the ground. Even though they had moved away from the tree she could feel one of its roots beneath the soil. It was so huge that her whole body lay upon it. It made her think of Strong way up among the branches. He was right in leaving me, she thought. But he shouldn't have done it the way he did. He shouldn't have singled out Jake and hated me because of him. He should have hated me for all my lovers, not just one. He knew I was a tramp when he fell in love with me. Maybe that's what he was supposed to do. Yes, that's the way it must have been. Oh, Tom, Tom!—you were my paraclete. You asked me to marry you, to have your children. If you loved me that

much, nothing should have made any difference, who
had had me, or how many. I know you didn't care how
many, but you shouldn't have cared about Peake.
Peake's nothing, he's not fit to shine your shoes. Maybe
if I'd said yes nothing would have made any difference,
not even him. But I didn't, Tom, and I'm sorry. I'm
sorry for being the way I am. But that's why you came,
isn't it? Because I am the way I am. Then you shouldn't
have forsaken me for any reason under the suns. Peake
was only a shadow that I walked through, that I'm
walking through again because he cleanses me of my
filthiness. Cleanses but does not cure me of it. But with
you beside me there'd have been no more Peakes. Ever.
I could have been what I was meant to be, a vehicle to
love you and to bear your children—not an unkempt
beast digging her fingers into the earth while another
beast paws off her clothes. Oh, Tom, Tom, Tom!

The buried root over which she lay pressed agonizingly upward into her back as Peake rolled upon her,
and she cried out in pain . . . and the pain blended
with the pain of her distress, and she cried out again
and pushed Peake away. She rolled over onto her hands
and knees. She was crying. "Marijane, what's the matter?"

"Go away, please go away," she said.

"But—"

"Go away!" she screamed. A long while later she
realized she was all alone beneath the tree. She had
fallen forward, and her face was pressed against the
damp grass. She had stopped crying. She got to her feet.
She did not think as she returned to the hotel, climbed
the stairs to her room. She kept her mind blank. Dead.
Her room was filled with ghosts. The ghosts of all her
lovers. No, not all of them. Tom's wasn't there. Without
undressing, she lay upon her bed and closed her eyes,
and the lovers went away. Sleep covered her like a dark
cloud.

VI

Yggdrasill astralis
Reproduction: Since this last giant tree is a female, the conclusion must be drawn that the species reproduced via cross-pollination. Unquestionably, some of the dead trees must have been male, and if they had not died cross-pollination would sooner or later have been effected, probably by the haha birds, with this tree or with one of the other females. Since there is no evidence of new Yggdrasills either in Kansasia or the rest of New America, such pollination did not occur previously, or, if it did, the fertilized seeds failed to take root. The absence of new Yggdrasills also indicates that reproduction via vegetation—i.e., the eruption of suckers in the vicinity of a respective tree—did not occur either, and strongly suggests that this species of tree does not possess this reproductive ability.

SHE stood tall and proud upon the plain. Her springtime leaves were like a new green gown.

She knew the sun, the wind, the sky. She knew the vast acreages around her. She knew the soil in which she stood and the life throbbing in her roots.

She knew the haha birds in her breast, and now she watched flights of them leave her foliage and fly far out into the new day, out, out, out, and disappear.

Below her, villagers came into the streets. They were

114

the Reapers. They went to this place and that, but most of them went to the steel sheds they had built, and flew out in little craft on missions over the dark-gold plain, flew out as the haha birds had, and disappeared.

The wheat was growing well. But not because of the Reapers who surveyed it. Because of the birds. Oh, yes, Matthews said in her dream. Because of the birds.

She felt the leaves of her springtime gown manufacturing sugar, and she felt her phloem carrying the sugar throughout herself. She felt the water the melting snows of winter had stored in the soil beneath her coming up through her sapwood. And knew a wrongness.

She understood what the wrongness was. And she thought, standing there in her gown of springtime leaves, I'm dying. I've been dying for years.

The dream-thought awakened Matthews. It was dawn. She lay in the pale premorning light, trying to remember what the wrongness was. As before when she had dreamed she was the tree, she could not.

How could I dream such a dream twice? she wondered. Both dreams were basically the same. And how could I have known something in both dreams that I don't know in real life?

But that was wrong. She did know it in real life—knew it without wanting to. Perhaps the knowledge itself was responsible for the dreams. Perhaps the dreams were her mind's way of hiding from her what she knew.

But what could she possibly know about the tree that she did not want to know?

Someone knocked on her door. It was Bluesky. "Matty? That time again."

"Right," she said, and got out of bed.

The dream still clung to her as she dressed. The haha birds, she thought. In the dream she had known something about them too. Suddenly she remembered. The wheat was growing well, but not because of the Reapers. Because of the birds.

The Reapers were merely watching the wheat grow, reconning it to make sure it had suffered no damage from the thunderstorms that sometimes walked across the plain. The haha birds were—were—

Were what?

She shook her head. She couldn't remember. Yet in the dream she must have known. She had said, Oh, yes, because of the birds. In the dream what the haha birds were doing had been so obvious that it hadn't even surfaced.

Nor did it surface now.

She washed in the lavatory in the hall, combed her hair, and went down to the dining hall. Peake and Bluesky were breakfasting at a table near the window. She saw no sign of the 3Vers. She got coffee out of the machine and went over and sat down at the table where her screens were. Should I contact Tom? she wondered. No. Perhaps he was still asleep. She would let him sleep as long as he could. He was lucky he was in the tree, she reflected, thinking of last night; of Marijane again brazenly walking out of the bar with Peake. If Owen had gotten the tree and Tom had been in the bar, she'd have walked out just as brazenly. This way, being in the tree, he didn't know.

The singing of haha birds again awakened Strong, but this time the songs were softer and lacked the sharp edges characteristic of haha birds' calls. Dawn did not greet his eyes when he opened them. Instead he saw candlelight flickering on an expanse of tree-ringed ceiling just above his head.

Remembrance overwhelmed him, and he turned his head, expecting to see the dryad's lovely face. He saw nothing but the artificial leaves of the aerial couch on which he lay.

He climbed down from the hammock to the floor. Except for himself, the grotto was empty. He donned clothes he could not remember taking off, looped his coiled saddle rope over his shoulder, and made his way through the fissure to the outside of the trunk. Genji the sun had begun to rise, and a few starved particles of its light lay upon the leaves around him. He walked partway out on the great limb that swept away from the fissure. Standing on the limb, he looked all around inside the tree. He saw blue blurs of haha birds above and below and all around him, but he did not see the dryad.

He remembered the name she had whispered to him in the night. "Xtil," he called. "Xtil!"

She did not answer. Perhaps she was ashamed.

No, it wasn't that. She loved him as much as he loved her. She had said so in the night.

"Xtil," he called again. "Xtil!"

Still no answer. But she would come to him again, he knew she would. She loved him.

He returned to the trunk and climbed down the bark to the next limb where the sack was. It was the next limb up from the lowest limbs, and, like them, it was a great horizontal sequoia. Had it not been so wide he could have seen down through the interstices of the foliage to the square.

He wasn't hungry. He got a vaccan of coffee out of the sack, opened it, and sat down on the limb with his back propped against a prominence of the bark. He lit a cigarette and smoked it between sips. He made plans. She would have to go with him when the tree was felled, she would have nowhere else to go, and she would want to anyway, because she loved him. "She'll be surprised when her tree dies and she doesn't," he said, "but she'll be able to take it in her stride. Hell, I'll be right there to help her." She was flesh and blood, the same as he. Maybe not all the time, but whenever she wanted to be. He lit another cigarette. Yes, she would come with him and he would protect her; maybe he

would take her to Earth and buy some strip of wounded
land that was turning green again and till the regener-
ated soil. Certainly he would make her his bride. He
would make her his bride, and they would be lovers always, the way they had been last night. "Yes," he said.
"Yes." And the old Tom—the one who had fallen from
the broken bough—would never rise from the dead
with his clotted misery, his pettiness, his conceit, his
fears, and the new Tom and his bride would be lovers
walking the lofty promenade of their love as free as the
wind that blew about them, as the stars that clothed
them in gentle light, far, far above the dingy under-
ground where the old Tom had written his wretched
life. And he thought and he planned, sitting there on
the limb in the green-gold morning light, the haha birds
winging around him, then arrowing out over the plain.

He failed to hear the smooth hum of the airhauler,
did not know it was in the sky till he heard Bluesky
calling to him from above the leaves. "Ready, Tom.
Ready when you are."

Strong jumped to his feet. The sooner he removed
her home the sooner she would come into his arms. His
lip transmitter and ear receiver were attached to his belt.
He put the unit in place and tongued the transmitter on.
"Send down the tongs, Owen. I'll meet them on that
topmost limb."

Rope coiled around his shoulder, he climbed up the
bark into the sunlight, marveling at the ease of the
climb. He drove a tree peg into the fissure before starting out on the limb, ran his rope through it and tied a
tautline hitch. Then he went out to meet the tongs.

He had to reposition the rope twice before he was far
enough out to affix them. He cursed the safety rules
Matty abided by so much. He didn't need the rope at
all. It took four cuts to remove the limb, and on the last
cut he had to burn two deep V's on either side of the

section so the tongs could get a grip. The limb gone, he split the trunk all the way down to the next limb and got rid of it with two huge horizontal cuts.

By means of more deep V's he also dispatched the next three limbs in four sections each. Then he split another sizable length of the trunk. The split near and at the top had to be wide enough for Bluesky to drop one of the jaws of the tongs inside the groove, and to obtain the width Strong had to turn the beamsaw to *Max* and back way out on the limb upon which he stood. He thought he made the cut wide enough, but when Bluesky tried to position one of the tongs' jaws, it became wedged in the groove. "Damn!" Strong said, and walked back to the trunk and without a second thought began climbing up one of the bark's deeper fissures.

"Tom! Stop!"

It was Matthews, who had dispensed with her usual "Good morning" and who up till now had said nothing.

Strong paused in the fissure and tongued on his transmitter. "Yes, Matty?"

"Tom, you can't climb a tree like that! What's come over you?"

"It's easy, Matty. It's like a ladder. It's the only way I can get up there to burn the tongs free. If I try from below, I might burn into the jaw."

"A ladder, hell! You've been up there too long. You're overconfident. Owen, put some more strain on the cable. Maybe the damn thing will come loose."

"Right, Matty."

The trunk trembled faintly from the winch's pull. Then Bluesky's voice again: "She won't come, Matty. More strain'll break the cable."

"Damn!" Matthews said.

Strong said, "Well, Matty?"

"There's a secondary stub up there. Can't you get your rope over it, Tom?"

"Sure, but it's nowhere near the top of the trunk. I'd still have to climb the bark."

"Well, get the rope over it anyway and get into your saddle. Give yourself some protection."

He descended to the limb, did as she had directed, then started up the fissure again. The rope was a nuisance, but Matthews was right. If he fell, he would not fall far. But if the fall injured him, the saddle would be worthless, for he would probably slip out of it. No matter. He continued to climb. It was not a long climb, and presently he came opposite the tongs' huge jaw. He climbed higher, till his upper body was above the severed top of the trunk. He half sat on it, his feet braced against a wide protuberance in one side of the fissure. His eminence provided him with a fine view of the world. The lower branches of the tree still concealed the village, but he could see the great dark-gold expanse of wheat, and the machine sheds and the incinerator and the crematory and the processing mill, and, far, far away, the long, long line of silos awaiting their surfeit of grain.

The airhauler was almost directly above him, its forward ventral camera tipped to hold him in view. He had expected to see the Haus Meiten too, but except for the airhauler the sky was empty. He could see Bluesky looking down at him from the winch doorway. Bluesky had already eased the tension on the cable; there was just enough now to hold the tongs reasonably steady when Strong freed the jaw. The jaw had turned slightly sideways and jammed itself in the groove at such an angle that an upward pull merely tightened the jam. All Strong had to do was widen the section of the groove that held it.

Such a simple matter. He got his beamsaw from his belt, turned it to *Low* and set to work, cutting carefully around the jaw. In a matter of seconds the jaw came free, and Bluesky instantly lofted the tongs so that the

slight swing freedom lent them wouldn't endanger
Strong. The swing itself didn't, but the freed jaw threw
the small section of wood he had dismembered straight
at him, and it struck the carotid artery in the left side of
his throat in a sharp ju-jitsu chop that lowered the curtains of his mind just long enough for him to lose his
balance.

Strong falling. He is conscious now, and the tree
seems to be growing at right angles to him, and just
beyond the treetop he sees the airhauler miraculously
holding a pair of gigantic tongs on a long outstretched
cable. The scene shifts, and now he cannot see the treetop or the airhauler or the tongs, he can see only the
bark up which he climbed a short while ago and along
which he is descending with demoralizing velocity. In
his left ear words materialize: "Tom! Oh, my God!
Tom!" Again his perspective has altered. He can see
now the huge limb toward which he is descending. It is
the same limb he left mere minutes ago. Is he falling
down toward the limb, or is the limb falling upward toward him? It is a perplexing enigma. Inches from the
limb (it seems) the slack of his saddle rope exhausts
itself, and the rope seat digs into his buttocks with such
force that, had he not grasped the other rope strand
sometime during his fall, his back would be broken. He
swings now in his saddle rope, marveling at the intense
blueness of the sky and the dark-gold beauty of the
wheat; rejoicing in the chinooklike wind that has now
begun to breathe across the plain.

Matthews's voice: "You all right, Tom? My God,
Tom, are you all right?"
"Sure, Matty," Strong said.
Peake's voice: "Thought we'd seen the last of you,
old buddy!"

"The tongs didn't hit you," Bluesky said. "What did?"

"That piece of wood I cut out." Strong touched the left side of his throat. It was sore, but the skin wasn't cut. "No damage done. Matty, I owe you. You saved my life."

"All you owe me is to finish the job without breaking your neck. To which point we're going to finish it a bit different than we planned. Even split, that trunk is already too big to handle aerially anymore and so are the limbs. So, Tom, after those two splits are gone you start dropping the limbs into the square. There's room enough, though you'll have to tip the lowest ones, and there's more than enough room to handle the rest of the trunk. Owen, Jake—after you drop the splits in the yard, land the airhauler. I'll meet you at the shed and bring you to the square. After Tom drops all the limbs and comes down, you two can get the trunk. Then you can cut everything to haulable size. Today, if there's time, tomorrow, if there isn't. You sure you're okay, Tom?"

"I'm fine," Strong said. "But I'll need another beam-saw. I dropped mine."

"There should be one in the airhauler. Is there, Owen?"

"Yes. There's one," Bluesky said. "I'll send it on down."

"Good. Finis and out."

You worked up now instead of down. The first limb Strong tipped was the one whose endmost burst of foliage hovered high above the hotel. Was it by this limb she had journeyed when she visited me in my hotel room? he wondered. Had she walked out to the end of it and then dropped fairylike down to his windowsill? No, he did not think so. He didn't know how she had gotten there. He had no idea how she moved about when no one could see her. Someday, after he took her to Earth and made her his bride, he would ask her. But it did not matter now. Now his concern was with the tree she lived in. Where was she now? he wondered. Was she still in the tree? He had looked for her on his way down to the limb but he had not seen her. Probably in that mysterious way she had of moving she had left the branches and gone elsewhere. Where, he had no idea, but it did not matter. Tonight, when he was alone in his room, she would come to him the way she had come to him last night in the grotto, and he would tell her then that he wanted her to be his bride. "Yes, I'll tell you then," he said. But right now, his concern was the tree.

The square was roped off from the village. Westermeyer's doing, no doubt. Well beyond the rope, tiny people were standing on the hotel lawn, looking up at him. There were other tiny people standing on the lawns of the flanking houses. Probably the square was surrounded by tiny people. He cut the limb about twenty feet back from the end, slowly so that the cut portion hung down at an acute angle before it fell. When it fell, haha birds streaked screaming from its foliage and winged out over the plain. They did not return. The cut portion seemed to drift down rather than fall. It landed well within the square. It was time now to cut the limb proper.

He had left his saddle rope at the limb's juncture with the trunk. Matthews would have had a fit if she'd known, but he had no mind to drive any more tree pegs than he had to, and besides, Matthews probably was picking Peake and Bluesky up at the airhauler shed. Even if she was on the scene, there was no way she could have known. He had to drive a peg now, though, and run his saddle rope through it so he could swing down below the limb for the undercut. He did so, tightrope-walking the edge of a prominence.

He turned the beamsaw to *Med* and made the cut, penetrating slightly less than half the girth of the limb. Then he went back up the rope to the top of the limb and began the final cut. He heard blurs of sound around him, and glancing up, he saw that the haha birds were leaving the tree.

Where would they go?

He remembered the words he had thought five days ago when he was standing in the square—*the tree was the last tree, and when it died the haha birds were doomed*—and a deep and terrible regret penetrated the armor he had built around himself.

A faint crepitation came from the limb. He continued to cut. "It's not my fault about the birds," he said.

He heard Matthews's voice. "Just got here with Jake and Owen, Tom. I can't see you, but I take it you're on the limb above the hotel."

Strong tongued on his transmitter. "Right." There were a series of foreboding creaks. "Here she comes!"

He stepped back and watched the limb part from the tree. The tree trembled. The cut he had made was perfect, but the limb did not fall on an even plane. Its much heavier inward section outpaced the rest of it to the ground. The impact of the base with the earth shook the tree again, and the *thud!* of the contact was awesome. Then there was a prolonged swish appended by a second, lighter *thud* as the remainder of the limb came to rest.

Strong's audience cheered. He saw two figures approach the fallen limb and recognized them as Bluesky and Peake. "Tom," Matthews said, "Owen and Jake are going to try to keep up with you. Whenever it's possible, do your delimbing as far from them as you can, and if you think they're too close, holler. And always holler before the limb you're working on is ready to fall. Better lock your transmitter on on-position."

"Right," Strong said.

"And for God's sake, be careful up there!"

"Sure, Matty."

He could see Matthews now. She was standing in front of the crowd on the hotel lawn. Not far from her, three other figures had also moved out in front. One of them was crouched behind an instrument Strong identified as a tripodic camera. Squinting his eyes, he identified one of the other figures as Marijane. Recognition did nothing to him, and he moved on to the next limb.

"We'd better move it, Jerry," Marijane said. "He's working his way around the trunk."

Without a word, Pruitt shouldered the tripodic camera and began walking clockwise around the square. Marijane and Dastard followed. Dastard was grinning. "What's the matter with Jerry, Marijane?" he asked *sotto voce*. "Cat got his tongue?"

"Shut up!" Marijane said.

She didn't like to think of the look on Jerry's face last night when she'd walked out of the bar with Peake again. It was too much like the look that had come onto Tom's face when she'd unthinkingly told him who her alley-lover was. Moreover, the contempt that used to rise to her succor in such instances had deserted her. Instead of being disdainful of Jerry's distress, she felt sorry for him.

Last night she'd dreamed the dream again, and this morning she'd once more overslept. When she and Johnny Boy and Jerry had breakfasted in the dining hall they saw through the window people standing on the hotel lawn gazing at the tree, and she'd known that now the action could be caught best from the ground.

Lots of pretty girls dream phallic dreams, she thought, walking with Johnny Boy behind Jerry.

Yes. But I'm a filthy old woman.

Looking up into the tree, she saw Tom's tiny figure circling the trunk. "Catch him," she told Jerry, and they stopped, and Johnny Boy helped Jerry set up the camera and they got Tom's progress on tape till he disappeared.

What is it with Tom? she asked herself as the trio resumed their walk around the square. Why now, after all this time, do I wish I'd said yes when he asked me to marry him? But she knew why. The return of the dream was why. The dream from which she'd thought her analyst had freed her. Only Tom could free her from it now.

He could free me from it with a touch of his hand. Tom, my paraclete.

She knew that what she was thinking was as much a product of her desperation as it was of her apostasy, that her paraclete was no holier than she. But she also knew that it was true. Tom, for all his foibles, had truly loved her, and if he could not forgive her, no one, nothing, could.

She lit a cigarette, but her hands were trembling so badly that she threw it away. God had trapped her with Tom. He had sent Tom to her, but He had tricked her into doing something Tom would hate, and then He had tricked her further by making her tell Tom what it had been. He had made it next to impossible for her paraclete to carry out his ordained task. Somewhere in her mind she had known these things when she had solicited Trans-Astralis for the big tree assignment. And now God had grown impatient. She had followed her paraclete to Plains, but only to deepen the wound she had already inflicted in him. Last night, beneath the tree, she had truly seen herself for what she was.

I'll go to Tom tonight, she told herself. If I must, I'll beg him to forgive me, first for taking Jake before him, then for all the children I've crushed. He needs only to touch me, and I'll know. . . .

* * *

Toward midafternoon, Strong dropped the last limb. The square was an abattoir of butchered wood.

He had worked through the noon hour, refusing Matthews's offer to send up a basket of food via his saddle rope. Now, in the limbless tree, he lowered the sack to the lowest limb stub. The stub on which he stood hid him from his audience, and he slipped into a deep fissure and climbed up to the stub that fronted the entrance to the grotto. He did not think she had returned, but he had to make sure. The grotto was empty; clearly, she had left the tree. The candles he had lit last night had burned down almost to their bases. In their fading light he went over and stood before the minitree and looked up at the hammock in which he and Xtil had spent the night. *If you haven't left the tree, come to me now,* he said, *and I'll tell you of the plans I've made, and then I'll take you down with me to the ground.* He listened, but no words that were not his own came into his mind and she did not bring her loveliness to brighten the fading candle flames, and he was certain then that she had left the tree.

He blew out the candlelight and returned to the outside of the tree. On his way down to the stub where the saddle rope was tree-pegged he heard Matthews's anxious voice. "Where are you, Tom? Tom, are you okay?"

"I'm fine, Matty," he answered. And then: "Owen, Jake—I'm going to send down the sack. Then I'm coming down myself."

He went down the doubled rope to the lowest stub, then he pulled the rope down, drove another tree peg, and tied one end of the rope around it and the other end around the sack. Then he lowered the sack to the ground. Fully extended, the rope was one hundred and sixty feet long—barely long enough for the task. After Peake and Bluesky removed the sack, Strong abseiled to the ground.

The audience cheered. Matthews ran across the square and kissed him. The ground felt strange beneath his feet. "Come on back with me and watch," Matthews said. "Now that you're back on earth the insurance clause no longer applies. Jake and Owen'll get the trunk."

"No," Strong said, "I'll get it."

He spoke the words flatly. Matthews looked into his eyes. They were focused on her face, but she sensed that he wasn't seeing her. "All right, Tom. It's your tree."

"When you go back to watch, take Jake and Owen with you."

". . . All right. Bring the sack, you guys."

"You okay?" Bluesky said to Strong.

"I'm fine," Strong said.

"Easy does it."

Bluesky grabbed one end of the sack, Peake the other, and they followed Matthews to the hotel lawn.

Strong stood in the square with the trunk of the tree and with its dismembered limbs lying about him. The trunk was not a trunk—it was the black core of a volcano, the earth eroded from around it. He had left room to drop it. When it fell, it would fall just to the right of the birdbath, at right angles to the hotel.

He turned and faced it. To drop it where he wanted it he would need a deep notch. He drew his beamsaw and turned it on *Max* and sent its XI-Gamma-16 particles darting into the wood. Into the bark and the bast and the xylem. He had to make the cuts wide so that the notch would fall free. When it did, he walked around to the other side of the trunk. The grass beneath his feet was dappled with the petals of tree flowers. In the slanted light of Genji the sun they were more than ever like drops of blood. He shuddered as he began the final cut. Straight across now. He cut deep. Deep, deep, deep. A groaning sound came to his ears as though from far away. It was the tree's. His audience had grown silent. Now the tree groaned again. There was a deep crepitation. He cut deeper. The trunk moved. Yes, it's going now. He had scuffed one of the tree-flower petals onto his boot. He kicked it wildly away. The tree shuddered, began its slow, sad fall. He moved well back from the trunk. It was like a mountain falling. *Tom!* someone cried. *Tom!* He looked wildly around. He saw no one except the people in the distant circular crowd.

There was a thick and thunderous sound as tree and ground collided at exactly the point he had aimed. The gasp from the watchers was a balloon of sound. The trunk quivered, then lay silently in the sun, and he walked around the great stump to where the fissured bark rose building-high. *Tom!* someone cried again. *Tom!* The "voice" was broken now, and he knew whose "voice" it was. He looked wildly down the length of the trunk. He saw a wisp of sunlight brighter than its surroundings. He began to run. The crowd of Reapers were shouting and dashing into the square, irrepressible in their delight. The people broke around him as he ran. When he reached the part of the trunk beneath which she lay, he knelt down beside her. *Xtil, Xtil,* he said. He could not see all of her—only her waist and breasts and arms and lovely, dying face. There was a fresh tree flower tucked in her hair. The rest of her was crushed beneath the trunk—her hips, her legs, her sandaled feet. *Xtil, I didn't dream you'd die!* he said. *You didn't kill me, Tom,* she said. *The inevitability did. Forgive me,* he said, and saw her smile and nod her head in such a way he knew there was nothing to forgive; and saw her die, and saw the grass where her head had lain, and the tree flower that had garnished her hair lying in the sun.

VII

A lavish smorgasbord covered end-to-end tables along one wall of the bar. Strong, who had never been in the room before, ignored the variegated array of food and went straight to the bar. He had showered but he had not shaved, and he had changed from tree wear to a white shirt, tan summer suit-slax, and dark-brown dress boots. He wore no tie.

The bar was full. Peake and Bluesky were there. They would move the dismembered remnants of the tree tomorrow. Matthews was there too. All had changed from tree to ordinary wear. Matthews even wore a dress. A white one. And there were Reapers. They filled not only the bar but most of the dining hall. Half the Reapers in the village, Strong thought. As he walked to the bar they cheered him. One of them patted him on the back and said, "The man who saved Bigtree!"

Matthews made room for him between herself and Bluesky. An Old Earth sat on the bar before her. Bluesky was drinking whiskey; Peake, Scotch. Straight. Westermeyer and Katerina were tending bar. The former ran to take Strong's order. Strong wanted Mary Muscatel. He wished he hadn't cut off his balls. "Whiskey," he said.

Westermeyer went to the top shelf. "The best," he said, filling a double-shot glass.

"Hey," Bluesky said, "my glass is empty too."

Westermeyer filled it and left the bottle on the bar.
"All of this is in your honor, Tom," Matthews said.
"I have no honor," Strong said. "I killed the tree."
"You could see them coming out of the horizon beneath the cloud of dust their hoofs threw up," Bluesky said, "and they were beautiful in their shaggy majesty and as dark and as magnificent as death."
"I know how you feel, Tom," Matthews said.
Strong drank his whiskey, refilled his glass. "No, you don't."
"I saw you crying beside the tree."
Strong said nothing. His hands lay limply on the bar. *What does a dryad do when her tree dies?* he asked, and she answered, *She dies too.* So you lie to yourself because you have to kill her tree, you pretend that she doesn't know, that she only thinks she's going to die. You pretend this because you love her and you have to kill her tree. "I have no honor," he said again. "I killed her tree."
"Tom!" Matthews said.
Strong fell silent again. He raised his eyes to the backbar, saw his mirrored self and shuddered, and then he raised them to the top shelf where his drink had come from, and finally to a shelf above it—the one where the Quantextil artifacts were stored. He saw a doll.
"Westermeyer!"
Westermeyer came running. "That doll up there," Strong said. "Let me see it."
Westermeyer had to stand on tiptoe to reach it. He handed it to Strong. "We found it here in the hotel when we were getting ready for the tourists," he said. "I think it had something to do with the Quantextil's worship of the tree."
Strong stared at the doll. It had been carved out of wood and been mounted on a small pedestal. It had been painted, and the paint was still intact. He stared at

the small, exquisitely featured face, at the tiny breasts that poked gently against the green, leaflike tunic, at the yellow, sunlike hair. At the long, slender legs. "I'd go so far as to say," Westermeyer went on, "that it represents a sort of goddess. A Goddess of the Tree."

"No," Matthews said. The wrongness of the dream had at last unmasked its horrid face. "It represents the Goddess of the Hearth."

"The Hearth?" Westermeyer said.

"Yes. The Hearth. Tom, don't you see it? It was there all along. The houses *are* the tree!"

Strong touched the doll's tiny shoulder. "Then why was she in the tree?"

"Tom, she was the Goddess of the Tree too. But she wasn't *in* the tree!"

"The hell she wasn't," Strong said. "I saw her. I talked with her."

"Get hold of yourself, Tom."

"Ms. Matthews, what do you mean?" Westermeyer asked. "What do you mean that the houses are the tree?"

"I mean that the tree grew them out of its roots. Just as the other trees grew their houses out of their roots. Grew them beautifully, enchantingly, to attract people. This species of tree, whatever species it may have been, needed people living around it in order to live itself. It needed the wastes people create, the dead bodies people bury. Recycled, that waste, those dead bodies, lent it the nutrients it couldn't live without. I should have guessed when the mill superintendant showed me the cross-section of one of the trunk sections. I did guess unconsciously, and that's why I dreamed—dreamed I was the tree. The thickness of the phloem, of the xylem—both pointed to the truth. That the tree needed more nutrients not only because of its great size but because of the houses. It had to feed the houses too. Don't you see, Doctor Westermeyer? Don't you see, Tom?"

Westermeyer's face had paled. Strong was still staring at the figurine. "But why are the houses rotting?" Westermeyer asked.

"Because you and the other Reapers improved the waste- and corpse-destruction facilities the later Quantextil had already employed. You not only continued the death rite, you upped its pace." Matthews turned and pointed to the rotted-out area in the farther wall. "That's a grave mark," she said. She faced the bar again. "Your houses are rotting because they're dying."

"Yes," Strong said, "she built the houses. She told me so. She was the Goddess of the Hearth as well as the Goddess of the Tree. But she was more than that. She was the tree. And I killed her."

"Tom," Matthews said, "snap out of it!"

"I'm all right," Strong said. "I understand all of it now."

Matthews said to Westermeyer, "The Quantextil who lived in this village saw what happened to the other villages and learned why, and they knew that the same thing would happen to theirs. That their tree would die and their houses would rot away. Maybe their tree lasted longer because they 'modernized' last. I don't know. But they knew that their tree and their village were doomed, and it was like having a god die. They didn't wait till it happened. They decided to die too. The blight, Doctor Westermeyer, was human stupidity."

"Tom," someone behind Strong said.

Strong turned. It was Marijane. He saw her face. It was the face of the woman taken in adultery whom the scribes and Pharisees had brought before Christ. *They said unto him, Master, this woman was taken in adultery, in the very act.* She said to Strong, "Please forgive me, Tom," and Strong saw that he had somehow killed this woman too.

He took her hand. "There's nothing to forgive, Marijane."

Marijane began to cry.

"Tom," Matthews said, "you're not the same."

"No." He put his arm around Marijane. "Part of me died up there in the tree." He faced Westermeyer. "There's more," he said. "The birds."

"The birds," Westermeyer said.

"Tell us about the birds, Tom," Matthews said.

Strong said, "The Quantextil worshipped the birds as well as the tree. I found evidence in the tree."

Matthews said, "Yes. The birdhouse."

Strong said, "And something else. There's a grotto in the trunk with paintings on the wall. The paintings tell the story. You can see them for yourself, Westermeyer, before the trunk is cut up and hauled away. The whole of Northwest New America is—or was—a biome. Each community of the biome was based on an ecosystem. The primary parts of the systems were the trees, the houses, the Quantextil, the wheat, and the haha birds. The trees housed the Quantextil and the birds, the Quantextil grew the wheat—probably not anywhere near the extent to which you people grow it, but enough to live on—and fed the tree with their wastes and their corpses, and the birds protected the wheat. The early Quantextil understood this and founded a religion based on the system. Probably they buried the religion in rite and ritual, and lost track of its basic nature. Anyway, the later Quantextil, who were relatively civilized, ascribed the customs of their ancestors to superstition, and in their blindness proceeded to divest the ecosystem of one of its vital feedbacks. Immediately the trees began starving to death, and eventually they died. Except this one. But this one was dying too, when I killed it."

Matthews said, "But what did the birds do, Tom? I know they fed on something in the wheat—I dreamed it. But what?"

Strong said, "I don't know. Plains locusts, perhaps—

or Plains grasshoppers. And probably on their larvae, too. Whatever insect it was, they kept its count down to unnoticeable numbers. I'll bet this'll be the last crop till the Reapers find out exactly what it was and devise their own means of suppressing it."

Westermeyer said, "My God." The faces of the Reapers within earshot had turned into gray stone.

Matthews said, "The tree must have been dying for years before the Reapers came."

Bluesky said, "Fifty million of them there were, living on the plains where now the Great North American Desert lies. And the grass they fed on was green and they returned it to the earth in their dung, and the grass grew green again. Fifty million! And when the white men finished, five hundred remained."

Strong said, "Matty, why was each tree planted almost exactly in the center of a great depression in the plain?"

Matthews said, "To obtain the maximum amount of water, I suppose."

Strong said, "Then someone must have planted them."

Matthews said, "The Quantextil?"

Strong said, "I don't think so." He looked at the figurine in his hand. "I think that in a way we can never understand they planted themselves."

Westermeyer said, "What're we going to do, Ms. Matthews? What're we going to do?"

Matthews said, "I think that everything's already been done."

Peake said, "What're you people talking about?"

Bluesky said, "Fifty million of them. *Fifty million!*"

Yggdrasill astralis
Former habitat: NW New America, Plains
(Genji 5)
Population: 0

ABOUT THE AUTHOR

Robert F. Young did not begin writing till his mid-thirties. He made his first sale to *Startling Stories* a few years before the magazine's demise. He has since sold to most of the science-fiction and fantasy magazines and has made sales to *Playboy* and *The Saturday Evening Post*. He has had two short-story collections published, and his first novel was published last year.

Young was born in a small town in western New York State and has lived there all his life, other than for the three and a half years that he spent in the army during World War II and during which time he was stationed in the Solomon Islands, the Philippines, and Japan. He has worked at various jobs, carrying on his writing on a part-time basis. He is now semiretired and writes full-time.

He is married, and his wife and he own their own house near the shore of Lake Erie. Since writing began as a hobby and took up most of his spare time, he has few others. He does considerable reading, particularly in the fields of psychology and ancient history. He enjoys writing science fiction because of the complete freedom the field gives to the imagination.

From DEL REY, the brightest science-fiction stars in the galaxy...